T0387546

THE WOMAN DIES

ALSO BY

AOKO MATSUDA

Where the Wild Ladies Are

Aoko Matsuda

THE WOMAN DIES

Translated from the Japanese
by Polly Barton

Europa
editions

Europa Editions
27 Union Square West, Suite 302
New York NY 10003
www.europaeditions.com
info@europaeditions.com

First publication 2025 by Europa Editions

Translation by Polly Barton
Original title: *Onna ga Shinu*

Library of Congress Cataloging in Publication Data is available
ISBN 979-8-88966-133-7

Matsuda, Aoko
The Woman Dies

Cover illustration © Isamu Gakiya

Japanese title design by Idea Oshima

Cover design by Ginevra Rapisardi

Prepress by Grafica Punto Print – Rome

Printed in the USA

CONTENTS

THE WOMAN DIES

The Android Whose Name Was Boy

The android whose name was Boy set out on an adventure. Setting out on an adventure had been programmed into Boy's memory at creation, and so that was what Boy did. Boy was the name the android had been given, and its appearance was indisputably that of a boy, but its gender was indeterminate. In what follows, therefore, we will refer to the android using the name Boy, and the pronouns it/its.

After walking for three days and three nights straight, Boy came to a small village and knocked on the door of a cottage that lay on its outskirts, its windows glowing with warm light. Being an android, Boy didn't experience tiredness, but it had been programmed to ask the old woman who appeared at the door, wiping her hands on the apron tied around her waist, if it could shelter there for the night.

The woman welcomed Boy inside and gestured toward a table beside the fire. Orange flames crackled in the fireplace. Watching Boy tucking into the soup that the woman had heated up, the white-bearded old man inquired,

"And what is your name, then?"

The wooden spoon that Boy had been raising mechanically to its mouth halted mid-air, and Boy replied,

"My name is Boy."

The look in the old man and woman's eyes altered in an instant. The woman's face tensed. She stood abruptly to her feet, her chair clattering, and took a couple of steps backwards. The pipe wedged in the corner of the old man's mouth dropped to the floor. Its ash scattered across the floorboards.

"A boy you say?" the old man said in a voice trembling with anger as he glared at the android. "If you're really a boy, then that changes everything. I'm sorry, but you need to leave immediately. I despise boys. We—we despise boys."

Standing behind her husband, the woman nodded in agreement as she wiped her tears with the corner of her apron. The fire snapped violently, as if sharing their emotion. Seemingly oblivious to Boy's placid expression, the man went on.

"A boy, you say! What do you take us for? We know exactly how this works. You turn up here, introduce yourself as a boy, drink and eat your fill, act all innocent, make us wonderfully happy, and then one day, you'll announce that an important mission awaits you, that you can't stay here any longer, and then vanish, just like that. Who knows what the exact reason will be this time? A dragon that needs slaying, or the arrival of a mystery foe, or some such. But whatever it is, we'll not hear a peep from you ever again. We've never even gotten so much as a postcard. Well, we're sick of it. We're two lonesome old folks—can't you just leave us alone? The older we get, the more it hurts. Although I suppose it's our own fault for building a house on the outskirts of the village, in just the sort of spot where boys like you are likely to lay eyes on it."

His gaze growing distant, the man looked out of the window. A tear slid down his cheek. The thunderous sound of the woman blowing her nose on her apron filled the cottage.

"Will you hear me out a moment?" Boy addressed the man and woman in a calm voice. "I'm not like the other boys that have come here. I won't do anything to hurt you."

It was the woman who spoke first.

"I know he says his name is Boy, but he does seem a bit different to the other boys we've met. He didn't gulp down his soup with astounding appetite, and he still hasn't had a second serving. He hasn't looked up at me with food smeared around his mouth in that way that perfectly rouses my maternal instincts, either."

The man fell into thought for a few seconds, then nodded.

"You might be right. Now that I come to think of it, he doesn't give you that piercing look right in the eyes like all the other boys."

"Let me prove it to you," said Boy, quietly. With empty bowl and spoon in hand, it walked over to the kitchen. Watching it go, the man and woman glanced at one another, their eyes wide with astonishment. The boys they'd encountered until now had scarcely seemed to know that such things as kitchens existed.

So it was that Boy came to live with the old man and woman. It was careful to ensure that all aspects of their life together were evenly balanced. It made sure not to behave in the sorts of boyish ways that delighted the old man and woman and made them look at Boy with their eyes full of love. It didn't get its clothes covered in mud, or lose its buttons all the time. It knew that it could be neither too perfect nor too imperfect, neither a child prodigy nor a problem child. Stray too far in either direction and it would become a boy. There was no secret surrounding Boy's birth, nor anything in its family that had been passed down from generation to generation for time immemorial. Boy harbored no dormant force that could be suddenly awakened by something or another, and it went without saying that it wasn't any kind of Chosen One. It had no intriguing scars or birthmarks on its body. It didn't allow its natural aptitude to spill out in everything that it put its hand to, or declare melodramatically that it had never chosen this destiny for itself. It didn't open its heart to the old man and woman, didn't reveal the loneliness it had always kept inside. It didn't fling itself into their warm embrace, telling them that they were its true parents. It didn't mature, either physically or emotionally. It was just around, in a steady, moderate sort of way. The key thing was the not-leaving. The not-going-off-anywhere.

When several years had passed, the man and woman gestured for Boy to sit down on the same chair on which it had sat on the day they'd first welcomed it inside, and said, calmly,

"You've proven your sincerity. We're grateful for everything you've done for us."

"Thanks to you, our image of boys has changed. Now we can go on living without sadness."

Boy nodded and said, "Okay."

The man and woman hugged Boy. Boy didn't hug them back as tightly, but they understood that it wasn't meant badly.

The following day, Boy set out from the village.

On and on, Boy walked. Its job was not yet finished. Whenever it got to a new place, it wrote a postcard to the old man and woman, letting them know its news. For the android, which had been programmed to do just this, this wasn't much of a burden.

Boy's journey continued. One day, it arrived in a village that was at war. Walking through the village, it came upon a girl sitting in shadow beneath the wing of a specially developed fighter craft, her eyes filled with sadness. When the Boy sat down beside the girl, she began to speak.

"And then before I knew it, it was me that was doing all the fighting. I was only supposed to be supporting him, but now it's me that's going out and getting injured, not him. Suddenly it's my role to protect the boy! And that's not the whole of it, either. I find these rash deeds of his so confusing. All around him people are dying, dropping like flies, but it's like he's guaranteed to live. Of course he apologises profusely each time I get hurt, but that's where it ends. He never changes in any fundamental way. I'm sick of it."

Boy nodded quietly.

From that day on, Boy started fighting in the war. Boy never showed any weakness or vulnerability. Regardless of the situation in which it found itself, it never grew overwhelmed. It looked on impassively at the atrocities of the battlefield. It didn't act recklessly, or come up with any far-flung ideas. It engaged efficiently in combat, avoided heroic deeds, and left the dying to die. Still, nobody lost their lives owing to Boy's actions. It didn't cause anybody any trouble, and wasn't saved by anyone, either. It didn't act big, and neither did it act small.

After several years, the war still showed no sign of ending. In the shadow of the fighter craft, the girl said to Boy,

"You've shown me that there are boys who don't behave like boys. I think I'm okay now."

Boy nodded quietly. The next day, Boy left the village.

Boy's journey continued. In every town and village in which Boy showed up, its name was mud. If people were kind to Boy at first, they'd always turn as soon as they found out its name, adopting a frosty attitude and speaking with sad expressions of the ill treatment they'd received at the hands of boys in the past. Boy listened to what they had to say, and stayed by their sides. Boy would spend at least a few years in each place. Sometimes it needed to remain for decades. For an android, though, that wasn't too much of a hardship.

Today, again, Boy is walking. The android whose name is Boy, developed to heal the wounds of those hurt by boys in the past, is on the move once more. Its patent is pending.

Bond

Today is a special day. Is this what you'd call a "social"? In any case, it's the first time for us all to get together in the same place. Is it presumptuous of me to say "us"? But no, you know what? It's definitely happening, so it's okay to own it. The world has acknowledged me as a femme fatale—so I tell myself to boost my confidence. I readjust my dress to ensure maximum cleavage, sweep back my golden curls with my palm, then stride into the hall on my long, slim legs and six-inch heels.

The large room contained the various generations of us. Not everyone was there, of course, but over forty were in attendance, chatting and laughing with slender-stemmed cocktail glasses in hand.

We were a captivating, glamorous bunch on any day of the week, but that evening we were particularly resplendent. The glinting chandeliers hanging from the ceiling looked crude in comparison. Glancing around that room filled with gorgeous women, it struck me that I was inhabiting the world I had always aspired to inhabit, and a feeling of deep happiness rose up in my chest.

Where had my initial confidence disappeared to, though? I found myself promptly transforming into a wallflower, gazing on in awe at the sheer elegance of my predecessors. But then a group of them noticed me, and with cries of "Ah, it's you!", welcomed me into their circle. Sure, we were calculating and out for ourselves only, would spare nothing to attain our objectives, and could be brutal if the situation demanded, but today was different. One flashed me a smile and said, 'If there's anything you don't know, don't hesitate to ask!", while another pressed a glass of pink champagne into my hand. Encircled by these women giving off such a staggeringly delightful scent, I felt as though I'd stumbled into a dream.

"So tell us, then. Is Bond really that good?"

At the sound of this lowered voice, everyone fell silent for an instant. The voice's owner, a woman with the sort of figure that could easily induce tears, was a newcomer like myself. Spotting me, she flashed me a diamond-white smile.

"Hmmm!"

"Well, I never expected to be asked that!"

The elder ones exchanged glances, slightly troubled expressions on their faces. Even troubled, they looked divine.

" . . . To be totally honest with you, I was a bit like, Oh, is that it?" said one woman, stepping bravely into the breach. Her chest-length cascade of light-brown hair glistened like a rainbow. "But I pretended like it wasn't that bad. I mean you would, right? It's Bond, after all."

The dam had broken. One after another, the others began piping up with their own thoughts.

"I didn't think he was so shabby! I actually found him pretty good," said a beautiful Asian woman with crimson-red lipstick, cocking her head.

"With me, it was all over in a second. I think he must have been tired," said a woman with a wildly sexy French accent.

"Yeah just between us, he's not exactly a long-laster, is he? But I guess he must get exhausted with so many missions to accomplish. All that stuff in the bedroom on top of that would be too much for anyone."

This woman had lustrous skin like molten chocolate, heavenly thighs and an ample chest. Oh, how transcendent we all were!

Our voices, which had started out hushed, gradually grew louder. There was drink involved and, above all, we had never had the chance to exchange information with one another like this before. How could it not be a riot? Maybe there would never be another such occasion again, meaning this was literally a once-in-a-lifetime opportunity. I plucked up my courage and hesitantly posed a question to my predecessors, their cheeks now charmingly flushed.

"You don't have to do it with him, do you?"

"I mean, of course you don't *have* to . . . but why do you ask?"

A set of emerald-green eyes framed by long eyelashes peered curiously at me. Inwardly fearing that what I was about to say was uncouth, I nonetheless puffed out my chest with its conspicuous cleavage and went on,

"I just feel like people are too quick to jump into bed with him. I mean, if they're into him then that's one thing, but there are times when they're obviously doing it as a way of getting him to lower his guard, which just feels a bit, like, dated or something? And even if there *are* feelings involved on his part, that's a hell of a lot of different people to be having feelings for. I just think there needs to be another way of impressing our beauty on people, do you know what I mean?"

As I was speaking, I felt my conviction swell. I wanted to create a different kind of us to that which had existed until now. Of course I had all the respect in the world for my predecessors. But times were changing—that much was indisputable.

"I don't know, I just feel like it's something you should try once," someone said, slapping me on the shoulder.

"Really?" I found myself replying, pulling a silly face. A titter went up from the circle.

"Just don't think too much about it."

"There's more prestige attached if you do."

"You might as well. You've not got anything to lose, have you?"

Now everyone began slapping my shoulders enthusiastically. There was a feverish sense of overexcitement in the room.

A woman with glasses, wearing a long dress that looked as though it had been painted onto her body, slipped up beside me. We were the kinds of women who were sexy even in glasses—no, we were *even sexier* in glasses. In a serious tone, she said,

"Honestly, though, I do think it's worth doing. The viewers will feel let down if you don't. Especially if you're the main girl. Then you should definitely do it. It's really shitty when the main girl doesn't—although it has happened in the past. Just think about it. You'd be disappointed if you were watching, no?"

Another with a voice so sugary sweet she could have spun cotton candy from it chimed in,

"Yeah, exactly. I didn't do it, but with hindsight I wish I had. It would have made for such a good conversation topic!"

"Right! It's way more fun if Bond screws around like crazy, and we screw around with him!"

What, exactly, was I being talked into here? As I felt my mind fog over for a moment, the other newcomer blurted out,

"If I'm honest, Q is way more my type."

Hearing this, our various generations of predecessors turned and pronounced in unison,

"No, you can't say things that! We'll lose our name!"

My eyes met those of the other newbie, and we burst out laughing. I wish you could have experienced what it felt like to be glared at so intensely by all those incredible women with such a wealth of experience.

Afterward, we carried on drinking and enjoying ourselves. Enough of the difficult conversation already! We were strong, sexy, and invincible. Bond was the only one who was any kind of match for us. Bond had to be led around by the nose by us, taken prisoner by our beauty, just as he always had been—that was how it had to be. It honestly sounded like so much fun. I couldn't wait until the day that I would get to finally meet him. Although if he turned out to be a total loser, then there was no way that I was going to do it with him.

Surrounded by all those strong and beautiful creatures, I felt myself truly proud to be one of them. When they began chanting, "Down it! Down it!" I gulped down my glass of champagne. Next there was going to be a round of Bingo.

Starry Night

I'm an early morning person. At this hour most of the other villagers are still asleep, but I blink my eyes wide open, my chest swelling with hope for the day to come, and light the lamp in my room.

I live in a little house in the center of the village. The house next door to mine has a red roof, but my house is without any distinguishing features—apart from its lamp being lit, that is. Close by stands a church with a tall, narrow spire, where my family goes on Sundays. The priest at the church is the same one who baptized me, and the fact I've now grown up seems to have escaped his notice entirely. He's not getting any younger, either, and has gotten very gray of late.

When I was young, I often used to ask my mom and dad,

"Why is my village different from other villages?"

That always stumped them. They'd look at each other, and one of them would say, "Hmm, that's a good question. It's just always been that way."

It seemed to me that they didn't really know the answer. So, I noted, there are things that adults don't know either.

The sky that stretches out above my village is not like a normal sky. Maybe there's no such thing as a "normal" sky, but this one is definitely a bit unusual. You don't find many like this in any books.

A few hours before dawn, I open the window and look up. The light from the stars is so incredibly clear, it's like looking at a patch of dahlias in full bloom. There's this one star that, with the glow extending all around it, looks like a huge white daisy. I think maybe my village is just really close to the stars. I haven't ever set foot outside of it so it's hard to say, but it seems possible that it's not actually on Earth. When that idea first struck me, I thought that maybe I'd made an amazing discovery so I asked my mom and my dad, but they both denied it. It's just a regular village on Earth, they said. Then my dad told me to stop talking nonsense and get down to my schoolwork, and pushed down on the top of my head with his big hand, firmly enough I thought my head might pop down inside my body and disappear. You can get toys that do that, right? Anyway, I gave them a look like I was satisfied, but in truth, I still find it kind of bizarre. When I'm a bit more grown up, I'll leave this village and then I'll solve the mystery once and for all.

I can hear the sound of insects from somewhere. I'm still looking up at the sky, by the way. I can't get enough of it, this sky that isn't like any other sky. My village is special, so it stands to reason that the sky would be special too. The light of the moon really is amazingly bright. It's a crescent moon today, but it looks like the crescent moon has been superimposed onto a full one.

I like it best when the sky looks like it's full of whirlpools, like it does now. You don't get that kind of swirly effect with normal skies. They're more pared back. The sky here undulates like waves do, with all these different colors. It sometimes reminds me of a sea creature or something like that. Or else, like a soul with something it can't quite bring itself to give up on. The sky in my village is super alive, just beautiful. When I'm looking out across at it, I feel the power to live surging up inside me.

When my neck starts to get tired from all that craning upwards, I look down and out across the village, still sunken in silence. There is one more weird thing about my village I haven't told you about yet, and that's the tree ghost that lives here. Of course I asked my mom and my dad why it was here, but their answer was as always: "Hmm, that's a good question. It's just always been that way." The tree ghost lives a little way away from my house. It flickers and sways like a great flame. All the kids in my village grow up being told by the village adults to keep away from it, and they do actually keep to the rules in that regard. Some of the older villagers go and make offerings and pray to it and things like that. I guess that's a kind of religion for them, in the same way that going to church is for us.

You might think I'm a wimp for saying this, but honestly, I'm relieved that there's a bit of a distance between my house and the tree ghost. I think it would be pretty hard to relax with a tree ghost slap-bang in front of where you were living. What if it decided to come and trample your house? What would you do then? The people living on the opposite side of the street from the tree ghost haven't said anything, but I figure they must be very on edge about the whole situation. But the tree ghost is really tall, tall enough that it is basically touching my beloved sky, so there's also a part of me that would really like to try climbing it. I don't have that kind of courage yet, but I hope one day that I will.

I turn and look absent-mindedly in the direction of the tree ghost, a bottle-green flame off in the distance, and that's when I first notice the person. They are standing at the window of a building on the far side of the ghost tree, looking this way. The light from their room, the only lit one in the whole building, picks out their shadowy form against the window frame. They can't actually be looking at me, I think to myself, but they are definitely looking at my village.

I'm pretty sure that building is some kind of an inn. They have roosters there that let rip every morning with their earsplitting crowing. It used to drive my dad crazy, that crowing. I wake up before the roosters, though, so it doesn't really bother me.

Still, it's rare for a traveler to be up now. I always get up at this hour, and I've never seen a light on in that building before.

This is the countryside, so none of the shops are open early in the morning. It must still be hours before breakfast is served at the inn.

I stand there watching the man. I think it must be a man. I can't make out his face properly, but there's something sort of rugged about his silhouette, a pointiness about his face.

The man isn't moving. He's just standing there, looking out, as if he's trying to commit the scene to memory. It's like he thinks he's taking a photo in the olden days, where the entire image would end up blurry if you moved at all during any part of the process—that's how perfectly still he is.

Maybe this man understands how great my village is, how incredible. My village with its whirlpool sky overhead and its resident ghost tree. It's quite plausible that he is overcome by how lovely my village is right now. Thinking that, I feel incredibly proud.

At some point I catch myself thinking that I wish this guy were a painter. It seems to me that for some reason, I could trust him to paint my village just as it really is. To paint it in all its specialness, without changing a thing.

The traveler and I stand facing one other, not moving at all. I lift a hand and try waving, though I'm thinking all the while that he probably won't be able to see it.

After a little pause, the man lifts his hand and waves back at me. The roosters at the inn have begun crowing, but he doesn't react at all. It's as if there is no sound in his world. Right at this minute, the traveler only has eyes for my village.

For a little while we stand there, waving at each other. We both know that soon enough, day will break, and our time will be over.

English Composition No. 1

"Is that a power suit over there?"
"No, it isn't."

"Is that a power suit over there?"
"Yes, it is."

"I see. So, is that also a power suit over there?"
"No. I'm sorry, but that's not a power suit. That's just a regular suit."
"Oh, really. I see."

"Was that a power suit, which the person who just walked past was wearing? I felt I could sense its power."
"No. I'm sorry, but that wasn't a power suit. That was just a regular suit."
"This is very difficult. How do you tell the difference between a power suit and a regular suit?"
"That's a good question. The defiant attitude of the wearer gives a clue. Also, if a suit has shoulder pads, it's more likely to be a power suit."
"I see."

"Is that a power suit over there?"
"Yes, it is."
"I think I'm starting to understand."
"Oh, really. I'm glad to hear that."

"Is that also a power suit over there?"

"No. I'm sorry, but that's not a power suit."

"Oh, really. In that case, maybe I don't understand after all. Power suits are difficult."

I Hate the Girls that You Like

I hate the girls that you like. The girls that you like are slender, dainty, and ethereal. The girls that you like never roar with laughter. You look down on girls who roar with laughter. Or rather, if a girl roars, then she is no longer a girl to you. Where should they go, then, all the roaring girls?

I hate the girls that you like. The girls that you like are fragile, defenseless, and incapable. What a klutz, you say, as you're overcome by the desire to protect them. They're not your children, and yet still you desire to protect them.

I hate the girls that you like. The girls that you like are selfish, fancy-free, and capricious as kittens. And yet, they make an exception for you. They heed every word that you say, so that everything turns out just as you want it to. We all know how little girls like to play with dolls, making them act out the various scenarios that they've dreamed up—well, the girls that you like are just like those dolls, that you do with as you wish.

I hate the girls that you like. The girls that you like catch on very quickly, have great potential, and respond well to teaching. The one doing the teaching is, of course, you. The girls that you like make you want to mobilize all your knowledge to educate them. They're not your students, and yet still you desire to educate them.

I hate the girls that you like. The girls that you like are delicate, artistic in their sensibilities, and feel things more keenly than other people. The girls you like shed tears at the cruelty of the world. Of course, a powerless girl like that has no hope of doing anything about said cruelty of said world. Yet still she bleeds, sacrifices herself, so as to protect you. At these times, your impulse to protect her has miraculously vanished into thin air.

The girls that you like never gain weight. The girls you like are light as a feather. The girls that you like don't grow hair anywhere other than their heads. Every inch of their skin is perfectly smooth and shiny. The crowns of their glossy heads are haloed in light. Their tiny chests, which have only just begun to swell, don't incite fear in you, aren't a threat in any way.

The girls that you like are clean, pristine, and transparent. Naturally they have no blemishes or scars. If they did, they wouldn't be the girls that you liked. Where, then, should all the blemished, scarred girls go? The girls with thick thighs and frizzy hair?

The girls that you like are all the same. They are like angels, like madonnas. They reveal their impish sides to you alone.

The girls that you like are mass-manufactured inside you. The girls that you like are freakish, like the girls in a Henry Darger drawing. At least that's how they seem to me. To you, they represent the correct form for girls to take. Other girls don't even register for you.

Occasionally, I picture the girls you like, the ones who do register in your vision, and am seized by an irresistible urge to doctor them a little.

To the girl perched elegantly on a chair, I add a pair of pince-nez. I remove the miniskirt and lacy blouse that accentuate the fragility of her frame, and put her in a pair of sturdy overalls. I give her split ends. I give her an anchor tattoo on her upper arm, like Popeye. I make that bicep ripple with muscle, so that the anchor tattoo really pops. I have her say the words that hurt you the most.

An Afro wig. A pair of geta sandals, for when she's walking to and from school. A putty eraser to chew on, in the place of gum. With little details like these, I go on mentally decorating the girls that you like. Hoping, as I do, that it'll make you disappointed in them. Praying that you'll be disillusioned by them. Because if that happens, they'll stop being the girls that you like. They'll stop registering for you.

In that world erased from your vision, the girls are free to get fat, get thin, run around, and laugh as they want to. There, in that paradise invisible to you, the girls are free.

Money

An ugly sense of foreboding flashed through the young man, and the next moment he realized his mistake. Making his way through the grassy plains, he had gotten into an altercation with someone from a rival tribe who'd happened to cross his path, and stabbed him. The tip of the young man's sword was lodged deep inside the enemy's stomach. It was an indisputable victory.

Blood poured like red spring-water not only from his foe's abdomen, but also from his mouth, which was opened as if in surprise. The young man hurriedly withdrew his blade from the other man's stomach, which only made the bleeding more severe. From the moment that the foe had fallen to the ground with a thud, he'd stopped moving entirely. A little way off, a crowd of vultures had already formed, eyeing up the corpse.

Ignoring their squawking, the young man inspected his sword. Yes, his premonition had been correct. It was the money one. He'd stabbed someone with his money sword.

Shit, thought the young man. Confusingly enough, both his real sword and his money sword hung from his belt. When the fight had broken out with the man, he'd reached for the first sword that his fingers touched, without checking properly which it was. From now on, he would have to take care never to let that happen again.

The money with which he'd stabbed his enemy glistened with blood. The young man looked around despairingly, but there was no drinking spot around these parts. Having little other option, he began to wipe his blade on the grass, attempting to get rid of at least some of the blood. What the hell am I doing, he asked himself. Wiping blood off his money like this made him feel utterly pathetic. If only it had been his real sword, the copious amount of blood he'd spilt would have been proof of his honor. The story would have spread throughout the village people as an example of a heroic deed. Hearing of his son's bravery, the young man's father would have declared him a real man at last.

After cleaning it for a while, the young man held up the tip of the money to assess it. There were some faint traces of blood still remaining, but the metal was copper in color to begin with so it wasn't that noticeable, he decided, giving himself a passing grade. It wouldn't do to waste too much time now.

The young man hurried on, his money sword once again hanging beside his real sword. It was unavoidable. That was the only place to keep them. The young man moved light-footedly across that huge expanse of land stretching out to the horizon, on which he had run around barefoot since he was a boy. Walking cleared his mind, so it was a good time for him to think through things. The young man had always loved walking across the plains.

Why was it that in his village, currency took the form of swords? It was such a pain. However you looked at it, having currency and weapons taking an identical form was impractical. Even before today, there'd been any number of times when he'd come hair-raisingly close to mixing them up.

Was that not the case for the other villagers, too? He felt envious of the adults who seemed unfazed by the situation as it was, whose calm expressions seemed to say that swords were swords and money was money. Maybe he was the only person in the village's history to have made such a blunder. He would have to keep it to himself, to avoid seeming desperately uncool. Nobody could find out about what had happened today.

Finally the young man arrived at his destination, the village general store. Batting away the flies mounting an offensive on either side of his face, he stepped inside the rustic, dingy shack.

"Good day to you." The sound of that luscious voice washed the bitter feeling of failure from the young man's heart, and filled it with sweetness.

The young woman who sat at the back of the shop was the most beautiful woman in the village, and the young man's first love. He came here frequently in order to see her. When he began listing off the items that his mother had requested, the young woman nodded and packed them into a woven grass bag. The young man was careful to take in each of the young woman's movements.

In response to the young woman's expectant gaze, the man hurriedly withdrew his money from his belt and handed it to the young woman. The young woman stared at the money that the young man handed her, then asked curiously,

"What are these spots of red?"

"Hm?" The young man felt his face flushing. To think that she'd notice! As he'd suspected, there was no fooling the most beautiful pair of eyes in the village. If he married this woman, his tribe would certainly prosper. With this thought, he felt his feelings towards her swelling even further. Yet at that precise moment, the woman's gaze changed to a menacing glare. The young man shuddered.

Having guessed from the young man's flummoxed demeanor the significance of the red patches, the young woman hurriedly changed her hold on the sword, gripping the tip of its hilt with her fingertips as if handling something sordid.

In a low voice, she said,

"Sorry, but are you taking the piss, or what?" The look she shot him was one of pure contempt.

So, the young man thought, this was how it all ended. His feeling was that of someone who had just been pushed off a cliff. Rock bottom, in other words. She would be sure to tell everyone of his mistake. People would know him as the greatest fool in the village, and now not only her, but nobody at all would want to marry him.

Seeing the young man's shoulders slump in a look of total dejection, the young woman said,

"Look, I won't tell anyone about it. It's not like you're the first, anyway. Although it's company policy not to disclose personal information about our customers, so obviously I can't reveal any more than that . . . "

With that, the young woman winked reassuringly at the young man.

So intense was the sense of relief that coursed through him that he felt he might burst into tears on the spot. Up welled in him the absolute conviction that this woman was the only one for him. Studying her, it seemed to him that she looked especially, exceptionally beautiful today. The necklace of colorful stones hung round her long, elegant neck suited her extremely well.

"I like your necklace," said the man.

The young woman's expression changed in an instant.

"This isn't a necklace. It's money."

She shooed him out of the shop. The young man turned back several times, casting wistful glances behind him, then began to trudge the long road home.

Why would you hang your money around your neck? Surely that was just confusing? Maybe the thinking behind it was using the neck as a kind of safe. But why? Besides, even if the necklace was money, it didn't change the fact that it suited her extremely well. Couldn't she just have received the compliment with gratitude? *That's some lovely money that you've got hanging from your neck*—would that have been the correct thing to say in that instance? Women were such fickle creatures. He would never understand them, as long as he lived.

Thinking this, the young man shook his head sadly.

Night had fallen across the plains, and a sky brimming with stars twinkled over his head. The young man decided to wish on them:

Please let money take a more easily distinguishable form.

Overwhelmed by the sense of his smallness, the young man walked on, a solitary figure beneath the lively night sky. His house was still a long way off.

You Are Not What You Eat

It was about four in the morning when I started puking. I'd not gotten to sleep until past 1 A.M., and usually, there'd be no way I'd be awake again by then.

I knew right away something was up. My body was heavy and sluggish, and my throat felt as though there were something stuck in it. At times like this, I'd always picture my body shrouded in a sticky, pale pink fog.

I stood up to go to the bathroom, and knew instantly I was going to puke. Resigning myself to my fate, I staggered unsteadily forward.

One of the good things about becoming an adult was developing a more constructive view of puking. When I was a kid, feeling nauseous indicated an Emergency Situation. The sense I had was that something totally disastrous was happening, and I'd turn not just physically white as a sheet, but spiritually as well. While I was throwing up, I'd be filled with terror that I might die. When it happened on a school trip of some kind, the embarrassment of it happening only to me would make me feel even more wretched. All those bitter memories of trying to grin and bear my nausea so my classmates wouldn't know. All those memories where I eventually puked regardless, the bitter taste filling my mouth. All those poor-old-me memories.

And yet, humans all puke from time to time, and once you've puked, the nausea goes away. No nausea is everlasting. Puking is a part of nature, a physiological phenomenon, and not a calamitous thing.

It was through the numerous parties that I attended since being of legal drinking age that I learned this truth. I'd like to express my gratitude toward everyone I met at that point in my life, for teaching me that. Still, it was incredible to me that all those little kids who reacted in such a nasty way to their classmates who'd been taken ill or become unable to suppress their nausea or their need to pee had suddenly as adults become so kind and open-hearted. Three cheers for the world of adulthood, where you can puke freely!

No sooner had I crouched down in front of the pristine white toilet seat than I felt something rising up from inside. Okay, here we go, I thought, opening my mouth.

The first part of puking was okay. Even as I gasped, I found that I still had the presence of mind to register the green and beige fragments floating in the toilet water.

That would be today's—or rather, last night's dinner: Babaocai that I'd had in a Chinese restaurant. 980 yen for a set meal, which came with rice and soup. The restaurant was in the shopping arcade outside the station, and I'd sometimes stop in on my way home from work. The interior was relatively chic, and it was the sort of place that a solo female diner could enter comfortably enough on her own. The green bits I could identify as the podded peas, and the beige as the bamboo shoots. The white lumps were as-yet-undigested grains of rice. The set meal came with a small pot of Chinese jelly, but there were no traces of that. That little spot of red might have been one of the goji berries serving as the garnish, though.

Past the age of thirty, this had started happening to me from time to time, even when I hadn't overeaten. I could only guess that my stomach was starting to get old, performing less effectively. Soon enough the nausea would end, and I'd feel better, I told myself. For lunch I'd gone with my colleagues for soba with grated yam, but I couldn't imagine we'd be going back that far in time. I tore off a section of toilet paper, ignoring the position of the perforated lines, and wiped my mouth.

Contrary to my predictions, though, my nausea didn't subside, and the next thing to emerge from my mouth were bits of soba. Had my stomach really been working as it should have been that afternoon? This seemed like incriminating evidence that it had been lazing on the job. Either that, or it had taken the afternoon off without telling me.

Taking the afternoon off was all well and good, but the act of vomiting took physical strength, and I began to feel tired. That morning I'd eaten nothing but a yogurt so soon enough, surely, I would start feeling better. The end to the nausea would come. You couldn't puke up that which you hadn't eaten, after all.

It was the luminous blue object I spewed up next which alerted me to the error of my thinking. The blue half-moon-shaped object was obviously an M&M. I could clearly make out half of the "m." The blue dye spread out through the toilet water like paint.

The thing was, I had no memory of eating any M&Ms—not just yesterday, but in the past six months. What need was there to eat M&Ms? Grown-ups had their own grown-up chocolate: the organic stuff, the stuff from New York that everyone was talking about, and so on. I was, after all, a grown woman. M&Ms? Don't be ridiculous.

It was true that I'd eaten a lot of M&Ms when I was young. My mother had disapproved because of all the artificial coloring, but at the time that lurid, energetic worldview had been oh-so appealing to me. Strange as it felt to recall, I'd been convinced back then that the brown M&Ms were better for me than the other colors. Brown was a calm, earth shade, and it was impossible to think that it was just as bad for me as the reds and yellows. For that reason, eating brown M&Ms would bring me a faint sense of relief. This, at least, I could justify to my mother.

Beset by another wave of nausea, I gave myself over to it,

only to find specks of those cheerful, familiar shades of orange, yellow, and green now dotting my vision. A few bits of what looked like popcorn, too. The inside of my mouth suddenly had the tell-tale taste of fizzy drinks. None of these were things I'd consumed.

As I vomited, I pictured a kid that I didn't know. A very kid-like kid, of the type I imagined would be likely to eat these sorts of things. The kid wore shorts and a baseball cap. On the kid's knee was a Band-Aid with superheroes printed on it, already peeling off at the edges. I knew from experience that those Band-Aids didn't have much adhesive power. I also knew that, as a kid, the cheaper a product was, the more you wanted it.

Anpan (with both white and red azuki bean fillings); chewing gum (the edible kind); cherries of a toxically luminous shade (thinking back to the taste of the fizzy drink before I guess that I must have been drinking some kind of cream soda)—the things that spilled out of my mouth were the comestibles of childhood. I knew it was hardly the time, but gazing down at them I found myself engulfed by nostalgia. It was like looking at a toy-box in miniature. I was half surprised not to find any shiny marbles and glass beads there.

Now the childhood stage gave way to a new phase. Up came leeks, onions, pumpkins, cucumber—an endless stream of vegetables emerged from my mouth. Honestly, this wasn't the most exciting of phases. Tomatoes, avocados, asparagus. The vegetables had begun to be digested, but they retained traces of the meals they had formed. Potatoes, cabbage, celery. There was no sight of any kind of dairy products, so maybe this person was a vegan?

My knowledge in this area being limited, my first association with veganism was Natalie Portman, but I assumed there was no way that my stomach could be connected in any way to hers. An image of her smiling broadly filled my head. Was this the time she'd received the Oscar?

The next thing to come up was a bit of fresh tuna. Natalie receded from sight. One might think it would be impossible in my current predicament to assess its freshness, but looking at the thickness and size of the freshly cut meat, I felt instinctively that it was very fresh. My mouth filled with the taste of the sea.

I called to mind the image of a rugged fisherman, carving up a tuna he'd just hoisted from the sea and eating it right there on the boards of his boat, seasoned with the soy sauce he'd brought with him. If he'd been able to fillet it there and then it must have been relatively small for a tuna. Large tuna were precious commodities. Depending on their size and weight, they could fetch millions of yen. I'd seen a thing about it on TV. After the tuna came a little bit of squid flesh, a beautiful translucent white, so I guessed the fisherman had also landed a squid into the bargain. The squid passed smooth and cool through my throat.

The food items eaten by this assortment of characters moved through my stomach and my throat before leaving my body. I remembered learning the proverb *You are what you eat* in an English lesson at some point. It struck me that if the person who'd thought that up could see me right now, they might change their mind.

Then came the cake phase (I could only think that the person in question had been to one of those cake buffets that were held at hotels); the convenience store phase (from the bento boxes to the various desserts, I could tell they were all 7Eleven items, and I had to agree that, given the exceptional range of desserts at 7Eleven, this was a wise choice); and the Hokkaido tourism phase (horsehair crab and sweetcorn-butter ramen). With each switchover, I would picture a new consumer. Quite possibly the involved parties were utterly different to how I imagined them, but for now there was nothing I could do to remedy that. Maybe when I was done I could search Instagram for pictures of people on holiday in Hokkaido posting pictures of horsehair crab and sweetcorn-butter ramen, people posting photos of themselves smiling with a plate full of cakes of the kinds that I'd just vomited up, but I guessed that there would be too many candidates to stand a chance of narrowing it down.

I had no clue why it was that I was puking for these people that I'd never encountered, but puke I did, on and on. Puking takes physical power. It's practically a sport. I wanted someone handing me sports drinks or honeyed lemons—although I guessed that I'd only end up bringing them back up again.

Around the point that it began to grow light outside, I realized that my feelings of nausea had subsided. Oh yeah, I recalled with familiarity, the ending came around suddenly. This purged, refreshed feeling was pretty great. I suddenly felt a bit dumb sitting there on the bathroom floor.

I stood up, in a daze. My face in the mirror didn't look particularly ravaged. On the contrary, I looked reasonably fresh—so fresh, in fact, that all that vomiting already seemed like a dream. I stepped on the scales to find that my weight was down by just 0.3 kilos.

My Secret Thrill

I draw a lot of pleasure from keeping the item whose ingredients I've run out of and which I therefore can't rustle up immediately on the menu, secretly fearing the entire time that someone is going to order it. You could call it my secret thrill.

Mine is a small restaurant, which I run by myself. It opens at 3:30 P.M., and closes at half ten. Three years in, I decided to stop serving lunch. Simple is best, I realized. The place is located on a backstreet, and neither the decor nor the food is that extraordinary, so it's really only regulars that come. The regulars have a particular way of ordering, as stipulated by the secret code observed by regulars the world over:

"The usual."

Time and time again, the regulars repeat this phrase. They sit in their usual seats, place their orders without removing their eyes from whatever newspaper or paperback or manga is open in front of them.

I know very well what "the usual" means for each of them, and I ensure that I'm never out of the ingredients to make those dishes. I have no problem whatsoever with "the usual." Simple is best, after all. And yet, I need to get my thrills somehow.

If worst comes to worst, I tell myself. I can always run to the nearby supermarket that's open until midnight. To date, though, nobody has ever ordered the item that I can't make, and I'm beginning to forget how to make it, which only adds to the thrill.

God Must Be Stupid

God must be stupid for not making cats immortal. That's an obvious design flaw right there. More than enough to turn a person atheist. Fair enough for humans to get sick, all things considered, but cats should not ail. Fair enough for humans to die, even, but cats should not. Cats ought to be indestructible. Cats ought be protected on all fronts, from all varieties of misfortune. A cat's coat should remain eternally soft and fluffy. It shouldn't grow coarse with age. It's a travesty for cats' bodies to become frail. Cats were intended to be leaping around eternally. Pouncing at the curtains, dashing across the tops of bookshelves. Cats, let us remind ourselves, are creatures so soft that they can slip right out of a human's arms and flow onto the floor. Creatures that can lie perfectly flat on the floor, yet the second they hear the call of a bird, the fluttering of wings from outside the window, go plunging at the window screen with an alacrity that makes their previous repose seem like a dream. Creatures that stare intently at the world outside the window. Creatures that calmly regard the morning. Creatures that calmly regard the night. Creatures that, when tickled above their noses or below their chins, make a purr that sounds remarkably like a gurgle. Creatures that pull their spine into a perfect bow-shape when stretching. Creatures that poop while staring fixedly ahead with a deadly serious expression—and then get the zoomies and go zipping around the room. Creatures that attack their food with perfect focus. Creatures that curl up into balls in people's laps. Creatures that, regardless of how long they've just played for, always want to play more. The benefits that cats bring to humans on a daily basis are fathomless. To repeat, whatever else might be permitted—the extinction of humanity, the explosion of Earth, etc.—cats should have been made immortal. Cats wouldn't mind if humans became extinct. They wouldn't even notice. Their instincts would impel them to set forth into space. Of course, being immortal, they wouldn't need spacesuits. They'd float gently through zero-gravity space with their front paws extended, journeying to new planets. Naturally the best outcome would be if they could find a new place of permanent residence, but the thought of them floating gently through space is enough to make humans squirm with pleasure. The thought of them passing through the Milky Way, tracing the course of the Big Dipper. The thought of them intercepting shooting stars with their front paws, and jumping on board. Cats will never die—just think how happily people would live, how happily people would die, were that the case. But as it is, humanity has to live in a state of unhappiness. God really must be stupid.

Thoughts on Balthus's *The Street*

That loaf of bread is so long

The National Anthem Gets It Bad

I remember the first time I noticed you. It was the enrollment ceremony, so it must have been April. They say that spring is the season for new encounters, don't they? But any excitement I'd ever felt toward the droves of fresh students in their identical navy uniforms that came traipsing in with the start of each school year had evaporated many moons ago. The students didn't have any interest in me, either. We kept our distance from one another: that was the understanding we had. I didn't fully comprehend what the issue was, honestly. I got the feeling that to them I was something unpleasant, which they were unable to avoid entirely.

The ceremony was proceeding according to plan, no hitches in sight. Soon enough, my turn rolled around. The teacher on the piano began playing, the students and teachers slowly opened their mouths, and the sound of me spread out to fill the gymnasium. The same boring old routine as always. Except, it wasn't. Something was different. Drifting over the tops of the students' heads, I focused all my attention on searching out the source of that irregularity. It didn't take me too long to locate. It was you.

You were the only one in the whole gym who wasn't singing me. Even when it's just one person, I feel it quite acutely. It hurts me, a lot. All the while that the others were singing, you kept your lips clamped firmly shut, your eyes pinned straight ahead. Your petite frame was positioned in the third row from the front, along with the other boys from year one, class two. On that floor that had been waxed until it glinted, you stood there looking somewhat at a loss, that delicate Adam's apple of yours unmoving. As my somber tones resonated around the gym, all I could think about was you. I liked the nape of your neck, so cleanly shaven. So began my love for you.

In the three years that ensued, I saw you only a limited number of times, but never once did you sing me. The less you sang me, the more I longed for you. I dreamt about the moment when your sound and my sound would resonate with each other. The feeling I got when I thought about your thin lips forming my shape seemed like it would be enough to stain the sheet music crimson.

What would I have had to be like, to convince you to sing me? What was it about me that you didn't like? Was it the impenetrability of my lyrics? How dated and uncool I was? Or were there other reasons? Would you have sung me if I was a hip hop track, if I was the latest smash hit? My crush was utterly unrequited. Unrequited crushes are lonely things.

And yet I also felt a sense of wonderment at the power of the resolve that you housed inside that small body of yours. Knocking up against this feeling of pride I carried toward you, I couldn't help but laugh at myself. You dazzled me, that was the truth of it.

Soon enough, the day approached when I had to bid you farewell. During the rehearsal for the graduation ceremony, the boy standing next to you noticed that you weren't singing me. "Sir, he's not singing!" rang his unfeeling voice through the gym. All the students' eyes were trained on your poor little body. The teacher got up from the piano and came over. "Why aren't you singing? Hm? You've got to sing!" Yet even then, you simply stood there, staring down at the floor. A volley of sniggering went up around you. The teacher clapped his hand down on your shoulder as if to say, you get it, don't you, then went back over to the piano.

Once more, the melody began. I guess you must have been intimidated by the scornful gaze of the students around you, because your mouth began forming the shape of my lyrics. If I said I wasn't aroused, I'd be lying. You were singing me! Just how eagerly I had anticipated this moment!

It wasn't long, though, before my elation turned to despair. You weren't, in fact, singing me. You were moving your lips to make it look like you were singing me. How piteous was the sight of your mouth flapping indiscriminately open and shut, like a goldfish in a bowl. And the cause of this deception you'd found yourself caught up in was none other than me. I had forced you to lie. The idea left me unspeakably miserable.

What the hell even was I? I thought of the others like me in the world. Weren't we supposed to be loved by everyone? Things would surely have been easier if I didn't have any lyrics, like my Spanish comrade. Then you could have just stayed standing there, not moving your mouth, without losing your pride. Thanks to me, you'd been hurt. The thought was unbearable.

The following day, clearly indifferent to the fact that I'd stayed up all night worrying about you, you didn't sing me. Your eyes glistening with resolve, your mouth pressed firmly shut, you stood with your spine perfectly straight, so much taller than three years before. Boldly and bravely you refused to sing me, and then you graduated. You were dazzling to the last.

Why is it that I always fall for the ones who won't sing me? My echoes still wrapped around the rafters of that now-deserted gymnasium, I traced the course of my various past crushes. You, sent off to war in a flurry of waving flags, your mouth sealed tight as a clam. You, stubbornly refusing to sing me despite your profession as a schoolteacher. You, standing on the soccer field, staring silently up at a fixed point above your head. What was going through all of your heads at those moments? I had no way of knowing. Love just doesn't seem to work out for me. It's really hard when your crushes never like you back. Sometimes I can't help but hate myself.

The Sky Blue Hand

Working on the production line, with my sky-blue rubber gloves on, I recalled the occasion that a sky-blue hand had waved at me. I was a junior high student at the time, on my way home from school. My schoolbag was heavy, my sports bag was heavy, and my uniform was heavy too. My mood wasn't exactly what you'd call light. Trudging along, I caught sight of a sky-blue hand moving by the hedge. I say a hand, but really it was more like a hand-plus-forearm, ending at the elbow. It had fingers and everything. The hand waved at me for a little while, with clear intent, and then disappeared. At that point in my life, I was still dissatisfied by how that particular shade got called "sky blue" when the sky was a lot of different blues and often wasn't blue at all, but still: the thing above the hedge was, indisputably, a sky-blue hand. In the gaps between the food items passing along the conveyor belt extending in front of the line of people all wearing the same white uniform and sky-blue gloves as me, I lifted a sky-blue hand and waved. Imagining my sky-blue hand hovering above a hedge or a post-box somewhere, greeting someone.

This Precious Opportunity

I'd like to take this precious opportunity to explain why I stopped licking the lids of my yogurt pots.

For many years, licking my yogurt lids was a secret indulgence of mine. I knew it was bad form, but if there was so much as a sliver of yogurt stuck to the foil it seemed a waste not to, and I'd feel restless until I'd done it. It was a guilty pleasure, through and through.

Every morning before work, I'd eat a small container of yogurt along with a slice of toast. I wasn't too fussy about the brand. In the supermarket, I would sling a few of those four-pot packs that crowded the shelves—plain, assorted fruit, aloe vera—into my shopping basket indiscriminately, which I'd then arrange on the shelves of my 118-liter fridge.

After opening the yogurt at the breakfast table, I'd lick the lid. Then I'd dip my spoon into the plastic container, move it to my mouth, and savor. Those little yogurt pots didn't contain much, and on occasion I'd find myself wanting a second.

When I was finished, I'd throw on my jacket, and the day would begin.

The end to these halcyon days of mine came around quite recently.

One day, as I licked the lid of my yogurt as usual, a message appeared:

Have a great day!

It seemed as though this particular yogurt manufacturer had decided to start printing messages on the undersides of their lids. It was plausible that they'd made that decision without ever entertaining the possibility that yogurt would cling there, but the effect was nonetheless that the words would be obscured by yogurt, becoming a secret message legible only to those who licked the lid. I was always taken by a guilty feeling as I licked my lids, as though indulging in some small transgression, and yet the message that had materialized was so unremittingly cheery that I couldn't help but feel sort of embarrassed.

All that was forgotten about in a moment, however, and I tossed my empty yogurt container in the bin.

The following day, the previous day's message wiped clear from my memory, I peeled the top off my yogurt to find another sprightly message greeting me:

Counting on you!

And who the hell are you, I thought to myself. Once again, the message left me with a feeling of discomfort, and I averted my eyes as I tossed the yogurt container in the bin. It ruined my whole morning.

The next day the message read:

Some days things don't turn out your way, but never give up!

Yeah, I'd known a few teachers and classmates who came out with this sort of superficial positive-thinking crap, I brooded irritably as I made my way to the bus stop, turning over incidents in my past that I had no wish to recall.

For the following few days, I ate the yogurts made by other brands which I'd bought at the same time, and licked their lids to my heart's content. There was nothing was written there. My pure, simple relationship with the lids remained uninterrupted, and my mood unspoiled.

Then came the fateful day. I woke up slightly later than usual and was in a rush, so when I grabbed a yogurt pot from the fridge I did so somewhat at random. From the underside of its lid emerged the line:

Did you lick it?

I was so enraged that I didn't know what to do with myself. It was as someone had stolen that clandestine joy that I'd taken in licking the lid, which I'd believed had been uniquely mine, and trodden it into the dirt. The feeling was that of being well and truly ridiculed.

Which is why I stopped licking the lids of my yogurt pots. I've been ridiculed enough in this life of mine, and I'm done with it. Now I exclusively buy Bulgaria-brand yogurt. The foil they use for their lids is made so that the yogurt doesn't stick to it at all, meaning I don't even have to manage the temptation to lick them. It's wonderful.

The Woman Dies

The woman dies. She dies to provide a plot twist. She dies to develop the narrative. She dies for cathartic effect. She dies because no one could think of what else to do with her. Dies because there weren't any better ideas around. Dies because her death was the very best story idea that anyone could come up with.

"I've got it! Let's kill her off!"

"Yes! Her death will solve everything!"

"Okay! Let's hit the pub!"

And so, the woman dies. The woman dies so the man can be sad about it. The woman dies so the man can suffer. She dies to provide him with a destiny. Dies so he can fall to the dark side. Dies so he can lament her death. As he stands there, brimming with grief, brimming with life, the woman lies there in silence. The woman dies for him. We watch it happen. We read about it happening. We come to know it well.

The woman gets married. She gets married to move the narrative on to the next stage. She gets married so that things can wind down to a nice finish. Not sure how to end it? Never fear! A wedding scene will always do the trick. Everyone loves a good wedding. There's really no better ending.

And so, the woman gets married. She gets married because they never really figured out how to develop her character. She gets married because she is no longer needed. She gets married because they couldn't be bothered to write a separate plot line for her anymore. And come on, what's so bad about that? She's married, for Christ's sake! She must be happy.

The woman gets pregnant. She gets pregnant to generate more drama. She gets pregnant so as to produce another character. When things are getting a bit stuck plot-wise, she gets pregnant to move the action forward. She gets pregnant to draw the story out. We are amazed at how her body suddenly swells up like that, how enormous her stomach becomes.

"Is this some kind of weird joke?"

"What is she, a human balloon?"

"What the hell is this?"

We whisper these kinds of things to one another as we watch.

As far as we can work out, all this is the doing of a mysterious white fluid. It seems unbelievable that a mere fluid could have such incredible potency (in fact, even now we still struggle to get our heads around this). It looks indistinguishable from any other cloudy white liquid.

There are those among us who already know that said white fluid is actually made by our own bodies, and whenever we visit Indian restaurants and they serve us a free lassi, it makes us feel pretty uncomfortable. Those of us who can't quite bring ourselves to touch our lassi on these occasions are given the eye by our parents, as if we were acting oddly. We stare at our mothers, gulping down their generous servings of white fluid, with abject fear in our eyes.

"Why aren't you drinking yours, honey? It's really good!"

From where we're standing, though, it's the mothers who are the odd ones. I mean, just imagine what they had to do to create us! The whole thing is unthinkably gross. And there's no getting out of it—you're either in the body-swelling boat or in the white-fluid-producing boat. It's one or the other. We begin to realize that we're going to have to live out our lives fully aware of our own biological grossness.

The woman miscarries. She miscarries to test the strength of the relationship. She miscarries because it's no fun when happiness is granted too easily. She miscarries because they can't make the film last two hours otherwise. Miscarries because the plot needs a bit of oomph. Her stomach suddenly deflates because they need to fill out the story somewhere else. We stare at it happening, shoveling popcorn into our mouths. We slurp down our Cokes and fail to understand what is taking place. We can still barely get our heads round how the woman managed to manufacture a baby inside her stomach in the first place, but the idea that the manufacturing process could somehow *fail* midway is really too much for us to digest. Why is the woman crying like that? Why is she having such a hard time with this? Our heads are filled with question marks. As we watch her break down and bawl, our mouths hang open. We don't get it, and yet we still absorb the lesson: *miscarriage is something that makes women cry, a lot.*

The woman miscarries. She miscarries so the happy ending will be more moving. She miscarries to lend a touch of tragedy to an already sad ending. Miscarries so that the man can get over the miscarriage, or so that she can. Miscarries in order that he (or she) can grow as a person. Miscarries so that he (or she) can move on. Miscarries so that we can see his (or her) face as he (or she) finally moves free of what's holding him (or her) back. Miscarries so that he (or she) can fall into a state of despair. Miscarries so that he (or she) can still dream of a brighter future, despite it all.

The woman is raped. She is raped so that the man can be angry about it. She is raped to spark his vengeful spirit. She is raped so the man can look to the sky and howl in agony.

She is raped so the man can have a car chase. Raped to bring about real action. Raped so the bad guy can be slowly but surely hunted down. Raped to put the man in the mood to blow up the enemy's hideout. Raped to make him feel like annihilating the enemy. Even we realize that this is a terrible thing to happen. We swallow nervously.

The woman is raped. The woman is raped at the earliest opportunity. The woman who was raped in the first installment is raped again in the second. She's raped like it's the only trick in the book. We feel a bit confused. I mean, it's clearly an unthinkable thing, and it drives the men into a frenzy, and yet they drop it in there at the slightest provocation. Why don't the men ever get used to their women being raped? Why do they make such a big fuss about it every time? We don't understand. We don't get that for a very long time, rape has been just about the only way they've been able to think of to wound and subjugate women. That it's the most comprehensible, most accessible method to hand.

The woman is raped. The woman is raped as a shocking plot development. We don't understand it, and yet the violent scenes traumatize us. It's so traumatic that even when we reach adulthood, we find ourselves replaying those scenes in our heads. Or else it's just hinted at. The woman's mouth is covered by the man's hand. The woman's body is covered by the man's body. The woman's face distorts in agony. Things fall. Things break. Crashing sounds. Windows shut. Doors shut. The light goes out. Cut to the next scene.

Confused, we turn to our parents.

"What just happened, Mom?"

"She was raped."

When our mothers finally answer, they are strangely casual, as if they're trying to tell us that it's really not a big deal, but they won't look us in the eye when they talk. It's not like the R-word makes everything suddenly clear for us. We don't get it.

That's precisely why we asked—because we don't get what rape is. Yet the look on our mothers' averted faces tell us not to ask anything else. Okay, we think. So this is a no-big-deal kind of thing. We are satisfied with that idea. If that's how it is, there's no problem. That thing that happened—that was just rape. The narrative continues.

The woman dies. She dies for the sake of a good story. The woman is raped. She is raped for the sake of a good story. We grow up watching it happen. We start not thinking anything of it, not feeling anything about it. Or maybe we were never that affected by it. Who knows? Anyway, now we are grown-ups, and we grown-ups are filing out of the cinema.

It was the late showing, and on a weekday too, so the cinema wasn't all that crowded. We'd seen a badly-made detective movie, and today, once again, the woman had died. She was the main guy's wife. Heard that one before? Yep, we have, as it happens. Though we all sat there facing the screen, all of us soon found ourselves pretty bored, and our minds moved on to various other things.

Of all of us, Kimiko was watching the most avidly, and not because she especially liked it, but because she writes a film blog. In other words, she was there with a mission: she had to find something—anything—to write about.

Yumi and Akira, both first-year university students, were happy as long as they could kiss and touch each other while the film played. For these young lovebirds, who'd only just got together, that was the main reason to go to the cinema.

Kenichi, whose well-hewn physique made him easy to identify as a construction worker, was fast asleep. Even he couldn't remember why he'd thought to see a film this late in the day. On the big screen, a man-turned-vengeful-demon was speeding underneath an elevated railroad track, causing all kinds of problems for the vehicles around him.

Hiroshi, who had a regular office job, was absent-mindedly imagining things. He was imagining what it would be like if, after the man rushed out of his flat in a righteous fury, the woman who had just died got to her feet, clothes torn and hair bedraggled, and heated up some frozen lasagna in the microwave. How she would then take it out and eat it on the sofa. The gaping holes in her chest rimmed in dark red. This was what Hiroshi always did without intending to. As he followed the story on screen, there was always one corner of his mind picturing the continuation of the scene that had just ended, as if it was a gateway to a parallel world.

Thus there was a place in Hiroshi's head where Luke was still dragging along his dead father's body, swathed in its black mask and long cloak. Hiroshi knew full well that the cloaked figure had by now already been cremated and everything, but inside his mental universe, that moment stretched on and on eternally. Through all the labyrinthine passages of the Death Star, through the forest, through the desert, Luke continues dragging his father's body. The flame of his life has expired, his cloak has turned white with sand, and Luke himself has reached the limits of his strength, yet still he continues to drag his father. His chest is heavy with sadness, and he has no idea where they will end up. When he imagines the two of them like that, Hiroshi feels tears pricking his eyes.

He didn't know what the dead wife, now tucking into her lasagna, would be thinking about. If only someone would phone the house, Hiroshi thought. If they did, then the wife would surely pick up the phone and say something. But in the absence of any such call, Hiroshi's imaginative powers reached their limit with the lasagna. As she made her way through her meal, her onscreen husband turned the Russian mafia hideout upside down.

And thus the crappy film came to an end, and we all left the cinema. We didn't know one another, so we walked at our own pace along the street that led in the opposite direction from the station. A cold wind was blowing, the residential area was quiet, and when we turned the corner, we found the dead woman. As we rounded the bend one by one, we each came to a sudden halt like a row of dominoes, almost tripping over our own feet.

The woman was lying face up on the ground. Much of her head was hidden by shoulder-length brown hair, but we could see enough of it to place her somewhere in her forties. Underneath her body was a great pool of blood. It was too small to call a *sea of blood* —it was more like a small pond. Which, going by what we'd picked up from films and TV programs, was not a good sign.

"Call the police," Yumi said to nobody in particular. She was pulling out her smartphone when the woman's hand twitched.

"She's still alive," Kenichi said, and, as if his voice had woken us from a trance, we all swarmed up to the woman, kneeling in a circle around her like vassals in a period drama. Yumi summoned an ambulance while Hiroshi called the police.

The woman looked as though she could die at any minute. Thus we learned that dying women really do look as though they are about to die. It was just like what we'd seen in the film an hour ago. In fact it was as if the woman who'd just died in the film had changed her mind, and decided to die out here on the street instead.

Come to think of it, this woman was not unlike the woman in the film. They had similar hair, and they were both wearing the kind of baggy T-shirt and sweatpants people usually wear around the house. This woman had apparently popped out to the convenience store. Close beside her body was a plastic bag containing a crème caramel and a toothbrush. Was the ice-cream container lying at the base of the utility pole anything to do with her? If it was, then the forensic team might be able to calculate the time of the incident by how much ice cream had melted. Akira thought about going over and touching the lid of the container to check the texture of the ice cream inside, but he didn't want Yumi to think him a fool, so in the end he stayed put.

The woman was looking more death-like by the second. It was hard to say what it was about her that gave that impression, but all of us there felt it. We said nothing, but we were all thinking the same thing: at this rate, the ambulance wasn't going to make it in time.

Before he could second-guess himself, Hiroshi found himself saying, "Do you have any last words—anything you want to say?"

We all felt that what he'd said was a bit impolite, but we could understand what he was trying to do. Taking our cue from him, we all started speaking to her.

"What happened to you?"

"Do you remember the face of the person that did this?"

"Is there something you want to tell your family? We can pass on a message."

We couldn't stop the woman from dying, but we could memorize her final words and pass them on to her loved ones, or do something to help solve the crime. Just that thought made us feel rather excited, in spite of ourselves.

" . . . something I want to say?"

The woman squeezed the words out, then suddenly opened her eyes very wide and stared at us. We were scared shitless. We wondered for a second if she'd become a zombie even before she actually died. Her fingers might have been trembling, but still Kimiko remembered to turn on the voice recorder of her smartphone. *The last words of the deceased.* The woman's family would no doubt thank her, tears streaming down their cheeks.

The woman inhaled. Her breath made a horrible wheezing sound in her throat.

"The thing I want to say is this."

We all swallowed.

"I wish I'd had the opportunity to deconstruct the vagina, at least once."

The woman said this in a single spurt, then closed her eyes again. Her hands fell to her sides, hitting the asphalt. We were totally mystified.

"Huh? Her VA-GINA?"

"Um, sorry, could you just repeat that? Did you say 'deconstruct'?"

The woman opened her eyes a crack, and looked at us as if we were a great nuisance.

"Excuse me, but were you raped?" Yumi said, as if inspiration had suddenly hit her. Her eyes ran the length of the woman's body. Then we all started looking at her, trying to check, but her thick gray sweatpants didn't show any signs of disarray. As we watched the woman looking at Yumi as though she took her for an utter fool, we sensed that the pond of blood beneath her was getting bigger.

"No! I just wanted to talk about the vagina, that's all . . . Okay, look, it seems like I've still got some time left, so I'll talk about it now."

"O—Okay."

We felt pretty bowled over by her energy—the energy of this woman who could well be dead in a few minutes. Kimiko thought about turning off the voice recorder but decided to keep it on, at least for the moment. From where she was lying, stretched out on the pavement, the woman began to speak.

"I've always found it so weird, how people make such a big deal about vaginas, you know? In the old days, of course, there was a great taboo around them, and women had to wear metal chastity belts and so on. Did you know that? Metal? Anyway, now it's all about liberation, so people go around saying that vaginas are beautiful and stuff like that, but the point is, who really cares if they're beautiful or ugly or what? Unless you do some crazy gymnastic moves with a mirror, you can never even really know what your own looks like. Talk about a design flaw! Seriously, though. Even if you look at your own face in the mirror every day, there's still no telling if you really know yourself, right? If looking at your face brought true self-knowledge, then nobody would need therapy, would they? I don't hate vaginas, and I don't particularly love them either. I think all this stuff about vaginaphobia is just stupid. Do people really believe all that? I'm sure they just come up with these big concepts to give themselves something to say—to feel important in some way. Vaginas are just vaginas. What's wrong with just admitting that? Don't you think?"

How could we possibly reply? We didn't have a clue what she was on about. Akira had still never seen a real vagina, and when he watched porn that part was always blurred out. Kenichi and Hiroshi had never properly looked at them either, just stuck in their fingers or tongues or penises as appropriate. Fingers were generally a safe bet to start off with—poke a finger or two in to begin with, and things mostly went off alright. Yumi vaguely conceptualized that part of her anatomy as a beautiful flower garden. As for Kimiko, if she had free time to think about her vagina, she'd rather put it to use watching films. And then writing up her impressions of those films on her blog.

We darted looks at one another. *Isn't this woman kind of perky for a dying person?* we were all thinking. Her voice sounded a bit too full of life for someone eking out the last of their strength.

"Aesthetically, I think they lack balance. In fact, just between us, I don't get how anyone can say they find genitals beautiful. Penises and vaginas are weird-shaped—grotesque, in fact! I don't get what's wrong with just admitting that. It's alright to have grotesque bits on your body, isn't it? I mean, I've looked at various people's penises and thought privately about how big they were, or how small, or about what weird-shaped things penises are to begin with. If those same people were looking at my vagina and thinking the same sorts of things, then so be it!

We both have funny-shaped things on our bodies. There. Can't we all just get over it?"

Won over by her fervency, we all nodded. This time we understood what she was saying a bit better.

We'd been trying to avoid thinking about that kind of stuff since we'd become adults, but there was no doubt that we did find genitals kind of gross. In fact, human bodies in general—both our own and other people's—were brimming with all kinds of icky functions.

"That's it. I've got nothing more to say."

The woman shut her eyes again and stopped moving entirely in a way that, after her previous bout of feverish energy, could only be described as sudden. As we stared on dumbfounded, we heard the sirens approaching from behind us.

In no time at all the woman was gone, carried away by the ambulance. Soon the spot was swarming with criminal investigators and members of the public wanting to know what was going on, but with its core component missing, the scene felt empty.

The police quizzed us about what had happened, and in unspoken agreement, none of us mentioned the vagina stuff. It was clear it would do nothing to help the investigation, and we didn't feel like we could reproduce what the woman had said correctly. Then we all left the scene, never having found out each others' names. We must have lived near to one another, since we all went to that same cinema, but our paths never crossed again.

Back at our respective homes we all, in our own time, obtained from the internet or the TV the news that the woman, who had been stabbed by a random street slasher, was now in a coma. We also learned her name.

At home, Kenichi fell straight into a deep sleep. He had to be up early for work again the following day. He really didn't know why he'd even gone to see the film in the first place.

Yumi and Akira slept together for the first time that night, and it was miraculously unterrifying. The moment they saw each other's genitals, they recalled what the woman had said, and laughed. The two teenagers, who'd really only just exited puberty, had never dreamed that they'd be able to laugh at their own bodies with such warmth as they did that night. Nor did they know that to do so was a feat most adults never accomplished.

Kimiko decided to leave the recording of the woman's voice on her phone for the time being. She didn't think she'd ever let anybody hear it, and she doubted if even she would listen to it again, but there was part of her that liked having the data there. She named the recording, and saved it.

Hiroshi ate a bowl of instant ramen as he looked at the news on his laptop. For the first time, he felt like he'd moved past the lasagna stage.

At the end of every day that passed, we'd check the news for developments. The police were still searching for the suspect. They recovered a knife that appeared to be the weapon used on a nearby riverbank. They didn't say whether or not it had fingerprints on it. There wasn't any news to say that the victim had regained consciousness, but neither was there any that the woman had died.

It's been five days now. At least she hasn't died yet.

How to Transform from a Punk into a Girl-Next-Door

1) Apply "Good Girl" blush by Addiction
2) Apply "Shy Girl" lipstick by MAC
3) Finito

(No need to change what you're wearing.)

How to Transform from a Girl-Next-Door into a Bad Girl

1) Apply "Deep Throat" blush by NARS (you can also use "Orgasm")
2) Apply "Dangerous" lipstick by MAC (you can also use "Brave Red")
3) Finito

(No need to change what you're wearing.)

Victoria's Secret

For as long as she could remember, Victoria had wanted to be a boy.

She'd never had any interest in all the things that other girls were into. She felt at home neither among the deluge of pinks and reds that marked out the girls' section of the toyshop, nor among the jagged silvers and blacks that made up the robots and model vehicles subsuming the boys' section. The color palettes seemed so starkly divided that she felt repelled by both options. Instead she would stand by the outdoor play section with its bouncy balls and hula hoops, gazing at the blues, yellows, and oranges—the plentiful variety of colors that coexisted there.

Victoria didn't dislike playing with dolls per se, but looking at the splay of pink boxes filling the shelves of their section she'd find herself quickly overwhelmed, until they all looked identical to her. Besides, she could never seem to find any dolls that wore the kinds of clothes that she herself wanted to wear. They were all fitted out in pretty dresses complete with lacy frills and ruffles, and the feet that finished off their slender legs were tucked away inside tiny plastic high-heeled shoes.

The dolls that Victoria liked were the ones dressed in various uniforms. She hadn't heard of utilitarian chic back then, but those plain clothes devoid of lace, frills, and ruffles seemed glorious to her eyes. Watching *Cinderella* for the first time, she much preferred the simple grey dress that the protagonist wore pre-transformation to the beautiful ballgown she was attired in afterwards, and her metamorphosis came as something of a disappointment. It was the same with *Beauty and the Beast.* She liked better Belle in the pale blue apron she wore at the beginning than in her lavish ballgown. When Beast reverted back to a blonde-haired man with a long jaw, her first thought was, Who the hell are you? In Victoria's opinion, he looked way cuter as a Beast.

There were a lot of things in the world, a lot of stories, that Victoria objected to. There had to be all kinds of exciting colors out there—why, then, did she find that so much of what was around her was either colored in grungy, boring shades, or else classified in overly simplistic ways? That said, she would occasionally stumble upon glorious stories, glorious colors, and at those times she would feel a burst of great happiness.

Into high school, Victoria began dyeing her hair assorted hues, wearing black jeans with holes and battered band shirts, and plastering her school rucksack with badges. She is now in her final year of high school.

Today Victoria—whose hair is currently a particularly vibrant shade of fuchsia, a shade which has finally allowed her to make her peace with pink—is walking around the only shopping mall in their rural town with her best friend, Teresa. They're here to shop for prom dresses, but Victoria isn't convinced about going to prom in the first place. Forking out several hundred dollars on the dresses of cheap satin and velvet of exactly the same design that were churned out every single year seemed dumb to her. She'd heard that the trendy kids would travel to the inner city mall by car to buy their dresses, so as to avoid turning up in the same outfit as someone else. That seemed dumb to her, too.

Passing by a lingerie store which shared her name, whose racks were festooned with lace underwear in shiny fabrics, Victoria averted her eyes in disgust. Seeing this, Teresa said with a grin,

"So what's your secret, then, Victoria? What are you hiding from your best friend?"

Since first becoming friends at middle school, the pair had come to this the mall together dozens of times, and every time they passed by this store Teresa made this exact same joke. Sometimes she would say it in a serious tone, sometimes feigning tears, but always messing around. It wasn't as if she thought it was funny any more—it was more that she'd always said it before, so she might as well now, for good times' sake. Victoria would come out with a different answer every time: *I'm actually an identical twin*, or, M*y great-grandfather was a vampire*, that kind of thing. Neither Victoria nor Teresa were into this kind of overtly sexy underwear.

Sipping on orange smoothies, they made their way through the mall. There were a lot of these kinds of scenes in high-school movies—the kind of movie where the cool clique in school takes a bookish girl under their wing and shows her how to dress ("you should lose those glasses"), so she can rock up to the prom or the post-prom party transformed beyond recognition. Unfailingly, Victoria would prefer the girls pre-transformation. Carrie looked good doused in pig's blood, she thought. Better that than joining the cool gang, and besides, there is something about her rage that's so cool. Victoria and Teresa's favorite movie was *The Craft*. It was the polar opposite to the usual world of pink that dominated—when the girl in *The Craft* transforms, there was an even higher ratio of black onscreen than before. The two of them had watched it in Teresa's basement, letting out squeals of delight.

"Maybe I just won't go to prom," Victoria found herself murmuring, as she gazed at the fountain and palm trees placed in the centre of the mall.

"Why? It's not like you have to go with a boy. At a small school like ours, it's fine to just go with friends. It'll be our last high school memory! I'll be sad if you're not there." Teresa put her arm round Victoria's shoulder and hugged her close. Teresa's hair is emerald green, the color gradually fading towards the ends. Of all the dye-jobs she's had until now, this is the most artful, the greatest masterpiece.

"I know, but I just really don't feel like wearing a dress."

"Why not? What about if you found a second-hand one? It'd be way cheaper, and you could see a bunch of movies with the money you'd save. It doesn't even have to be a dress. We could both go in purple suits, like in *Mean Girls*."

Teresa was all ready to make for the nearest exit, but Victoria held her back. And then, a moment later, before she could really process what was happening, she found herself confessing her secret for the first time in her life.

Teresa's eyes, already plenty large, grew perfectly round. Taking a firm hold of Victoria's shoulders, she shook them firmly as she said.

"But why the hell would you want to be a man, Vicky? We're constantly talking about how stupid and helpless men are. The boys at school are bad enough, but they're even worse when they grow up and get out into the world, trust me. I don't want you to be a man."

Needless to say, Victoria understood Teresa's feelings all too well. She herself was thoroughly fed up with the boys at school—or, more accurately, she was thoroughly fed up with everything at school.

"I promise, I won't become a tedious, manlike man. But I'm just—I'm just done with it. I don't like my name. I want to be a man and have a name like 'Victor' or 'Spencer' or something."

"Like Dr. Spencer Reid in *Criminal Minds*? He's totally amazing. I don't think I'd mind if you turned out like him, actually. I was already thinking it was kind of messed up that there was only one of him in the world."

For a brief moment, Teresa's eyes sparkled and she looked at Victoria with a rapturous look, apparently already seeing her as a future Spencer Reid. As if an IQ of 187 was ever in the cards for her.

"He's definitely cute. I dunno . . . Now I've said it out loud, I don't even know if that's it, exactly—I don't know if it's that I want to be a man. It's like, I've always felt like there's something different about me, and I can't put my finger on what it is."

Victoria tossed her empty smoothie cup in the trash, and wiped off her fingers on her jeans.

"I get that." Teresa passed her hands through her emerald green hair several times, mussing it up, then tied it up with a rainbow hair tie. On her neck was a temporary tattoo of an anchor.

"It's so tedious, isn't it, the way so much is already decided from the get-go. I'm totally on your side though, so whenever you want to come out or whatever, I'm always here for you. I don't really even know where my own sexuality is at."

Come out—the words repeated themselves inside Victoria's head. What would happen if she were to come out now? She felt a sense of discomfort toward her gender, but it wasn't like she was into other girls, and in fact there was a boy that she had her eye on at the moment. How all that stuff would pan out in the long term, she had no idea. How did you categorize someone like her? And what should she do if she changed her mind along the way? Come out again? Try to be accepted by a different group?

She didn't really know, and nor did she understand why the impetus was on people like her to do the coming out. Didn't they have things to come out about too? Things like, *I'm actually prejudiced*, or, *I've actually never once donated money to charity*, or, *I actually write abusive things about people online every day*. Why did they just sit there and wait for others to do the coming out to them, as though they themselves didn't have anything in their lives that warranted such a move? If coming out was such a brave thing to do, then they should get involved.

Then she could have applauded them, and actually meant it. If you didn't come out then you couldn't be seen for who you were, and it meant you were hiding something—was that how it was? God, why was everything in the world so crappy?

Walking through the parking lot, Victoria threw her arms above her head. If only her arms were longer, she'd could have swirled the clouds around. Teresa grabbed hold of Victoria's hand, swinging it back and forth vigorously like a swing with a very energetic child on it, and said with a smile,

"Victoria doesn't have any secrets. Okay?"

The Year of No Wild Flowers

Wild flowers grow in fields. Wild flowers grow along roadsides. Wild flowers grow by railway tracks. Wild flowers grow beneath trees. Wild flowers grow in corners. Wild flowers are mostly small, flowers whose form you can recall only vaguely, born into this world at random. Wild flowers frequently come in pale colors: white or pink, sky blue or yellow. Sometimes they come in bold colors, extending their serrated leaves and long, thin stalks toward the sky.

Plumed Thistle

A member of the daisy family. A perennial herb that grows on flat or hilly terrain. Stems grow to between 50 and 100cm, their lower regions densely covered in white hair. Basal leaves, which endure while the plant is in flower, are 15 to 30cm in length and cleft to form 5 to 6 pinnacles. Tough thorns of length 2 to 3mm protrude from the leaf margins. The flower heads are made up of disk florets. Bracts are oblate in form, the 6 to 7 sepals stick straight out, with strips of mucilage on the underside of the outermost leaves. Corollae are 1.8cm to 2.3 cm across, made up of five deep crimson petals.

Wild flowers grow on riverbanks. Wild flowers grow by the water's edge. Wild flowers grow in cracks in the asphalt. Wild flowers walk along asphalt roads. Wild flowers live in the places whose stations only the slow trains stop at. Wild flowers live in studio apartments whose doors don't have autolock. Wild flowers write on their calendars. Wild flowers occasionally forget the garbage days. Wild flowers sing in the bath. At the end of the day, wild flowers eat a salad and sandwich that they bought from the convenience store and remember as they're eating, that they had exactly the same thing for lunch. Or else, they're tossed about by the wind in the fields, and remember nothing.

Shepherd's Purse

A member of the mustard family. A very common annual herb that grows in full sun on flat land, characterized by its triangular, flat seed pods. The stem grows from 10 to 40cm tall and, as with the leaves, is covered in sparse hairs, some of which are stellate. The basal leaves are usually deeply incised, with the deepest incisions at the tips. Several sessile pointed leaves grow at the base, hugging the stem. Flowers have four white petals about 2mm in length, while its seed pods, known as silicles, grow 5 to 8mm long, with stems of 1 to 2cm.

Wild flowers aren't special, or peculiar. Wild flowers are everywhere. There's nothing unusual about wild flowers, nothing that merits noting. Wild flowers are always positioned to one side of the classroom, of the office. You find wild flowers somewhere on every bit of land, in every building. Wild flowers wear the same uniform as you. Wild flowers wear a different uniform to you. Wild flowers truly are everywhere.

Persian Speedwell

A member of the plantain family. A down-coated biennial herb found growing in sunny, flat grassy areas or along roadsides. Stems branch diffusely from the base to grow prostrate, becoming erect toward the tips, where they grow to a height of approx. 10cm. The leaves are 1 to 2cm in both length and width. Inflorescences are borne singly from the leaf axils, forming more densely at branch apexes. Petioles are 1.5 to 4cm long, while the 4 sepals are 6 to 10mm long. The corollae are approximately 8cm across, made up of four azure petals with dark blue lines. Seeds are about 1.5mm across.

You pass wild flowers in the corridor, on the stairs, in the supermarket. Wild flowers are sitting next to you in the doctor's waiting room, on the bus. Wild flowers blend into the darkness at your feet on your way home. Wild flowers peep from the cracks in the walls. Wild flowers were there beside the bar of the level crossing that your train just passed. Wild flowers got their prescription two minutes before you in the drugstore.

White Clover
A member of the legume family. A common perennial that grows in fields and along roadsides, it is entirely hairless. Stems are long and creeping, rooting at the nodes. Leaves grow alternately, each consisting of 3 leaflets. Leaflets are between 1 and 2.5cm in both length and width, edged with fine teeth, usually with a white, hooked pattern. Flowers are borne from the leaf axils, growing taller than the leaves, about 2cm across. The five petals are white or pinkish in color, and 8 to 10mm long. The calyx splits into 5 sepals around halfway up, which grow to around the same length as the pedicel. The seed pods containing 3 to 6 seeds are 4 to 5mm long and encased in dried petals.

Sometimes you turn your head when see a wild flower, sometimes you stop walking, but only ever momentarily. There are more important things in your life, and you forget about the wild flowers almost immediately. That's how it is with wild flowers. You don't need to worry. The wild flowers don't blame you for it.

Southern Rockbell

A member of the bellflower family. A perennial herb that grows along roadsides and in grassy fields. Stems grow 20 to 40 cm tall and ridged, branching at the base to grow in clusters. The basal and lower leaves are oblanceolate, 2 to 4cm long and 3 to 8mm wide, sinuate with thick white margins. Flowers are borne at the apex of a long stalk, and have five lanceolate sepals 2 to 3mm in length, which are persistent. The corollae are 5 to 8 mm long, funnel-campanulate, with quinquepartite blue petals. Fruits are 6 to 8mm long, obconic.

Wild flowers don't tweet. Wild flowers don't connect. Wild flowers don't give likes. Wild flowers don't upload photos of the pancakes they're about to eat. Wild flowers don't put their everyday thoughts and discoveries on the internet where the general populace can find them. In one sense, then, wild flowers don't exist in this world.

Buttercup

A member of the buttercup family. A perennial herb common in sunny fields. The hollow stem grows to 30 to 60cm tall, entirely coated in erect white hairs. The basal leaves are wider than they are long, at 3 to 8cm in width, splitting halfway or further up into 3 to 5 lobes. Five-petaled bright yellow flowers 1.5 to 2.5cm across form at the end of 3 to 7cm stalks. The 5 sepals grow to 5mm long, their outer surface covered in erect hairs. Petals are around 9mm in length, with a single nectary at their base, their undersides pale yellow. Stamens and pistils are numerous. Fruits are bifid, 2 to 2.5mm long with slightly hooked tips, clustered into orbs.

That's pretty rare these days, no? People say this to wild flowers a lot, but they don't really understand why people would do that all stuff, why they would *want* to do all that stuff.

Suddenly everyone around them had started doing it—that was more or less the extent of their thinking about it.

The majority of people don't know what wild flowers are doing, or thinking. What they like, and what they don't. Of course they don't know. If wild flowers wanted people to know those things, they'd have to allow those things to be known. They'd have to make an effort. They'd have to sign up to whatever it is online. It's kind of strange to think about: that if you don't put in the effort to make yourself visible, if you don't promote yourself, then you don't get seen. That you end up not existing. Do they really want people to know that stuff about them?

But what people?

And what stuff?

Wild flowers don't know what it is that the world wants to know about wild flowers. So wild flowers don't move their mouths. So wild flowers don't move their fingers.

Asiatic Dayflower

A member of the dayflower family. An annual herb growing in flat or hilly fields and meadows. Stems grow from 15 to 50 cm tall, branching diffusely from the base and grow prostrate, becoming erect toward the tips. Leaves are 5 to 7cm long, 1 to 2.5cm wide, and ovately veined, forming a short, membranous pod at their base. The pods have long soft hairs at their openings. The bracts are around 2cm long, wide and cordate, folding inwardly, with a rounded apex. The inflorescences are subtended by modified leaves called spathes. The flowers are about 1.2cm across, opening outside the spathe. There are three sepals, those on either side of the flower join at the base and are mucillate. The uppermost two petals are large, round, and violet in color, growing erect; the other petal is small and white. Two of the stamens are pollen-producing, while the other four are staminodes. The fruit are round, white, and fleshy, forming three valves.

On their break, wild flowers go to the nearby bakery to buy bread. Passing beside them is a car with capabilities unlike that of wild flowers. The wild flowers' coat flaps with the motion of the car. Wild flowers don't cut up their apples, they bite into them whole. Music comes spilling out of wild flowers' ears. Wild flowers guffaw at comic strips. Wild flowers stroke a passing cat. Wild flowers are stroked by a passing cat. Wild flowers are trodden on by running shoes. Wild flowers are picked. Wild flowers become part of a flower garland. Wild flowers wear a flower garland. Wild flowers wear a new hat.

Blue-eyed Grass

A member of the iris family. A perennial naturalized in grasslands near urban areas. Leaves grow 4 to 8cm long and 2 to 3mm across. Flower stalks reach 15 to 25cm in length, with narrow, flattened wings. Bracts are 2 to 3cm long, and linear pinnate or broadly linear. Pedicels are 3 to 4cm long, with flowers around 1.5cm across. Tepals are roughly 1cm long, ovate-oblong, and either pale purple with darker purple stripes or solid maroon. Flowers have 3 stamens. The fruits grow 3 to 4mm tall, oblong or spherical in shape, glabrous, and brownish-purple when ripe.

Wild flowers look up at the sky. Wild flowers count the stars. Wild flowers weigh out the correct quantities. Wild flowers make proper miso soup from scratch. Wild flowers eat McDonald's hamburgers. Wild flowers fall in love. Wild flowers don't fall in love. Insects land on wild flowers. Insects feed on wild flowers' nectar. Strange secretions emerge from wild flowers. Wild flowers open. Wild flowers wilt. Wild flowers' seeds are scattered on the air. Wild flowers get angry. Wild flowers get disappointed. Wild flowers get sad. Wild flowers rejoice. Wild flowers hate. Wild flowers love.

Viola Mandshurica

A member of the violet family. A common, stemless perennial that grows in dry, sunny conditions in fields and mountains. Often covered in fine hairs. The upper half of the petiole is winged. The leaf blades are 3 to 8cm long and 1 to 2.5cm wide, widening toward the bottom. Pedicels are 5 to 15cm long, and petals 12 to 17mm. The side petals grow white hairs. Spurs are 5 to 7mm in length. Sepals are 5 to 8mm long, with toothless auricles. The capsules are hairless.

Wild flowers grow beneath the metal staircase leading up to the ramshackle wooden apartments. Wild flowers grow next to the red postbox. Wild flowers put letters into the red postbox. Wild flowers receive letters. Wild flowers read the letters they've received. Time passes. Time goes on passing. Time passes in no time at all. At the end of the year, wild flowers think about how long they'll be able to go on living like this. Or else, they're tossed about by the wind in the fields, thinking nothing.

The police detectives blanched when they first laid eyes upon the crime scene, newly transformed into a lake of blood, but it transpired that none of the cats had been harmed. As a resident cat sidled up to one of the detectives' feet, mewing loudly, he smiled in spite of himself.

We Can't Do It!

We can't do it!
We can't do the things that we can't do!
We can't do the things that we're not suited to!
We can't be forced to engage in tedious conversations!
Because tedious conversations are tedious!
We can't smile along while people boast endlessly to us of their achievements!
We can't sit there and say, wow, that's amazing!
We can't satisfy their cravings for the limelight!
We can't be modest and unassuming so as to put everyone at ease!
We can't make ourselves humble!
Because there's no need for us to!
Because it's not our duty to!
We can't "take a back seat!"
We can't "be behind our men!"
Because we can't be bothered!
Because it's stupid!
Because it's a total waste of our time!
We can't tolerate sexist behavior!
We can't accept this sexist society of ours!
Because that's not the kind of life we want!
Because enough's enough!
We can't do it!
We can't do the things that we can't do!
There's no way in hell we can do it!
We'd sooner die before we do it!

Toshiba Mellow #20 18-Watt

Those are the words I would have loved for someone to whisper in our ears, when they saw us standing there so lost and forlorn in the lighting section of the DIY store.

Hawai'i

The sweater that hadn't been worn for three years was sipping a glass of tropical fruit juice by the poolside. The glass was so large that, in order to lift it, the sweater had to cradle it with both of its arms, where its wool had begun to pill. In addition to a straw, the drink had some kind of exotic flower and a brightly colored cocktail umbrella poking up from the rim, so even just looking at it fostered a holiday spirit. Every now and again, though, the sweater would mistake one of these other items for the straw and come close to sucking on it. When the sweater had first arrived here, it was so enchanted by the little cocktail umbrellas that it had rescued each and every one and carried them back to its hotel room, but, predictably enough, that phase had now passed.

From its suite on the top floor of the luxury hotel, the sweater that hadn't been worn for three years could look out over the great expanse of emerald-green sea. It was there that every morning, stretched out on the crisp white sheets of the enormous bed, gazing up at the sky through the window, the sweater ate its room-service breakfast: eggs Benedict, yolks oozing out onto the gleaming white plate, washed down with freshly squeezed orange juice, and a café au lait to finish. The room was kept at exactly the right temperature, making it a most pleasant place to while away the time.

In the pool, the floral-print dress bought on sale but never worn and the white shirt owned in quintuplicate were floating together on a giant inflatable killer whale, chatting animatedly as they trailed their sleeves in the glinting water. In the lazy river a little way off, the long patchwork skirt that no longer fit its owner's lifestyle was lying atop a float. It had mentioned a little while back how it wanted to brush up on its swimming.

No sooner had the sweater that hadn't been worn for three years drained the last of its tropical fruit juice with a loud slurp than a fresh one was brought over on a tray, boasting a different colored exotic flower and cocktail umbrella than before.

Wasting no time, the sweater that hadn't been worn for three years picked up the new drink and took a sip. It was almost too delicious to be real. How many different kinds of tropical fruit juice did they have in this place? Since its arrival, the sweater had drunk at least one each day but had never been served the same kind of juice twice.

"Ahhh, this place is utter paradise!" the sweater that hadn't been worn for three years said with a contented sigh.

It was speaking the truth. The place really was paradise.

"What kind of paradise would you prefer?"

The sweater that hadn't been worn for three years remembered how stumped it had felt when the angel first posed the question. It had never given the matter a thought. The handbag whose design was now so outdated and the CD whose owner figured they could always just buy it again in the unlikely event they ever felt like listening to it looked equally at a loss for words. The three of them shot worried glances at one another.

Perhaps this was a common reaction, for the angel seemed to immediately grasp their bewilderment and set about explaining the decision facing them in a voice as light and airy as meringue.

"You can choose whatever kind of paradise you like. No need to feel shy about just speaking up and telling us exactly the kind of place you'd like to spend your time. Of course, if you get a bit tired of a particular heaven, you're free to switch at any point. Some even choose to spend their time in a different paradise every day. The choice is entirely yours. Our priority is for you to feel safe and happy after undergoing such cruel treatment. We have a catalogue here showcasing the options, for your reference."

The angel opened up the thick catalogue that had materialized out of the blue right in front of them.

Sure enough, the range of paradises available was truly extraordinary. There was a skiing paradise that was all slopes and snowy mountains, and a paradise set in the middle of the jungle. There was a paradise for those who loved picnicking amid the cherry blossoms, a paradise modeled on an amusement park, and paradises with themes like *Around the World in Eighty Days* and *Lord of the Rings*. For those who preferred a more classical model, complete with winged cherubs holding bows and arrows and frolicking atop marshmallow clouds, that option was also up for grabs.

"You'd be surprised how many end up going for this one in the end," said the angel with blonde ringlets, giving them an earnest look.

"I'll take this one," said the CD you could always just buy again in the unlikely event you ever felt like listening to it, pointing indifferently at the Northern Lights paradise on the page opened before them. The sweater that hadn't been worn for three years found itself wondering whether the CD wouldn't find it a little tiresome, given the similarities between the aurora borealis in the picture and the CD's own reflective surface. Of course, it wasn't really any of its business to be worrying about such things, but that didn't stop the sweater that hadn't been worn in three years from feeling a pang of disappointment on the CD's behalf.

"I'd like to try this one," piped up the handbag whose design was now so outdated, pointing at a Disneyland-themed paradise that was permanently in Halloween Party mode.

"Oh yes, that one comes particularly highly recommended,"

smiled the angel, before turning her gaze on the sweater that hadn't been worn for three years.

And before the sweater knew what was what, it found itself uttering the word "Hawai'i."

Hawai'i—the place that the girl who hadn't worn the sweater for three years had always yearned to visit, her number-one dream destination.

Back when the girl still wore the sweater that hadn't been worn for three years, she would often devour magazines that included features about Hawai'i with hungry eyes, taking in every detail. The sky and the sea. Stacks of pancakes so tall that a person had no hope of finishing them alone. Shopping malls lined with designer shops. The lip creams and chocolates you could buy at the local supermarkets and take home as presents for friends. Organic cosmetics that weren't available in shops in Japan. When the girl's chest throbbed with excitement at the sight of these things, the sweater that hadn't been worn for three years could feel it too.

Then, with the same degree of obsessive passion, the girl threw herself into decluttering. She began mercilessly to ask herself whether her things sparked joy, and then to toss them away.

It was evident that something was up right away. The girl would roam around her flat with a look of intense focus, darting glances in all directions like a ruthless dictator determined to drag each and every one of the citizens from their hiding places. The mugs of which she owned more than ten. The stylish paperbacks in English she'd only ever flicked through. The music box she'd treasured since she was a child. The shoes she hadn't worn for two years. The folding umbrellas, of which she had three. The little trinkets and ornaments that lacked any coherent purpose. Nothing, absolutely nothing, escaped the girl's razor-sharp gaze.

The leather jacket she'd bought because it was the kind of thing her ex was into. The shocking-pink miniskirt she had no idea why she owned. The socks and the tights of which she had over thirty pairs. The T-shirt whose collar had stretched with age. The girl opened the closet and inspected each item of clothing with a grave expression. *Can I live without this? Is it high time I got rid of this? Do I really need this in my life?* The look in her eyes as these questions went reeling through her head was petrifying.

As objects vanished from the flat one after the other and the rooms began to grow ever more bare, the sweater that hadn't been worn for three years had a dim sense that it was destined to meet the same fate as the others. After all, it had been three years. And lo and behold, that was what had come to pass.

"I'd like to go to Hawai'i," the sweater said, in a tone more certain than before.

"As you wish," smiled the angel.

And yes, the Hawai'i where the sweater that hadn't been worn for three years was sent may have been a Hawai'i-themed paradise exclusively for objects purged in the name of decluttering, but it was still great. The sweater liked it very much indeed. Although it should perhaps be mentioned that thus far the sweater had ventured no farther than the poolside. Tomorrow, it would tell itself most days, tomorrow I really will get out and see a bit of the island. But in the end, lying by the poolside drinking tropical fruit juices generated such a deep sense of satisfaction that the sweater kept putting off any excursions. Tomorrow it really would get out and about a bit. It wanted to check out Diamond Head, see what that had in store. The sweater that hadn't been worn for three years wondered if its former owner ever did make it to Hawai'i—if all that decluttering had somehow freed her up to go.

A towering stack of pancakes topped with a mountain of whipped cream appeared beside the deckchair where the sweater that hadn't been worn for three years was sitting. The sweater took a bite, and the sweetness of the maple syrup scored a direct hit to its brain. Reeling with contentment, the sweater gazed up at the sky. Up there, not far from the rainbow, the pair of skinny jeans owned in three similar shades was paragliding together with the dress worn once to a friend's wedding and never again.

The Purest Woman in the Kingdom

Once there was a prince who wished to marry the purest woman in the kingdom. Such a woman must not only be a virgin—that went without saying—but never have come into contact with any man except for him. Only a woman of this kind would make a suitable match for a prince like himself. Concerning the all-important virginity issue, the ideal thing would have been to ask a doctor to verify this medically. However, if the women had gone and had their hymens restored, it would render any such examination meaningless.

What a pain these medical advancements were, the prince thought to himself. Yet he understood well enough that one couldn't assess a person's purity with one's eyes alone. However beautiful a woman was, she may turn out to be a slut. Appearance wasn't always the best judge of character. The prince knew of several such real-life examples of this. His mother, in fact, was one. There was no damned way he would allow himself to be deceived by a woman. What, then, should he do?

After three sleepless days and nights, the solution finally came to the prince. He would rely on technology. The prince visited the laboratory where the foremost scientific technician in the kingdom worked, and spoke with him. Upon hearing the prince's request, the technician nodded, saying quietly, "As you wish, your Highness."

Two months later, the item that the prince had requested was finished. He immediately sent out a notice that all the women in the kingdom should be summoned to the castle. He didn't give a reason.

Reclining leisurely on his ornate throne in the sumptuous reception room of the castle, the prince donned the glasses that the top technician in the kingdom had created for him. He gave his retainers the nod, and the grand doors in front of him promptly opened. A line of women began to file inside.

The special glasses that the prince had ordered were such that they glowed to indicate which parts of the women's bodies had ever been touched sexually. If a woman's hymen had been repaired, he'd know the truth immediately. *A fantastic invention, if I do say so myself*, the prince had taken to muttering under his breath. Forgetting that it was the technician who had created the glasses, he was thoroughly intoxicated by the ingenuity of his idea.

Now, all was clear as day. The areas where the women had been sexually touched were revealed to the prince as patches of light. Their chests, their genitals, their bottoms, their faces—various parts of the women's anatomy glowed. Even the most innocent-looking of the young women before him weren't without some illuminated zone. *Well, well, well,* the prince thought to himself. Delighted, he dismissed young woman after young woman with a flick of his right hand. After a while, his wrist grew tired.

To avoid revealing his intention, the prince hadn't set any age constraints on his summons, and so the stream of females that appeared before him included both the very young and the very old. Laying eyes on old women whose entire bodies glowed in a manner standardly described as saintly, the prince found himself a little shaken. What kind of filthy lives had these women led, for goodness sake?! Generally speaking, the number of illuminated body parts increased as the women's age did, but the prince was surprised to see children not yet ten years old glowing in places as well. Heavens, but the women in this kingdom were corrupt! Despair washed over the prince. It didn't occur to him that sexual touch potentially encompassed a whole range of different things: being groped, raped, sexually abused, and so on. But even if he had realised this, the prince's conclusion would likely have been the same: such a woman wasn't pure. And that was all that mattered.

With each and every woman that appeared before him glowing in some manner, the prince started to get fed up. Why did women have to be so disappointing? At this rate, he was going to have to marry the princess of the neighboring kingdom that his father was pushing for. Such a high-ranking woman was bound to be arrogant. The prince was determined that he should choose his wife for himself.

Eventually the end of the line came into view. There were fewer than ten women left. Utterly worn out, the prince was thinking about how eager he was to get back to his room and watch some online porn when the last woman stepped up.

Having come to believe that such a thing was impossible, the prince didn't register at first that no part of her body was lit up. Not so much as a speck of her glowed. Thinking that maybe his glasses had clouded over, the prince summoned the retainer waiting close at hand, and bid him to wipe the glasses with a velvet cloth.

The prince returned his glasses to his face, their lenses now gleaming, only to confirm that the woman standing in front of him and hanging her head bashfully was totally unilluminated. A miracle! What was more, she was beautiful! A pale-skinned face, and pink lips. Her silky brown hair flowed down nearly to her waist, and her ample chest seemed ready to burst the buttons of her white dress open. He had found her. The prince had found the purest woman in the kingdom! But of course he had: he wasn't a prince for nothing.

The following day, the prince married the woman. He didn't

bother checking whether or not she wished to marry him. That wasn't how princes did things.

Finally, their much-anticipated wedding night rolled around. As the two lay side by side on the enormous bed, the prince went to kiss the arm of the woman that he'd just married in her white negligee, but the woman pulled her arm away. Oh, she's shy! the prince thought to himself happily, and went to touch her again. It was then that the prince felt a bolt of sharp pain across his cheek. Astounded, he looked in the woman's direction to find her standing by the bed, fists raised in a fighting stance. Piecing things together, the prince surmised that he had been punched by the woman.

Leaping from the bed in anger, he made to fly at the woman, but reading his moves, she drove a fist into his stomach before he could get there, and then, with a movement as fast as an antelope, brought her heel crashing down upon him. Collapsing onto the Persian rug at his feet and feeling its texture against his cheek for the first time, the prince began to cry in pain. This was not the kind of thing that was supposed to befall a prince.

It was at this point that, in a most unexpected turn of events, words of apology began to rain down on the prince from above. I'm so sorry, Prince. I can't tell you how sorry I am. It was the first time he'd heard his wife's voice, delicate and melodious as a bell. The prince had no idea what was going on. As he lay there, physical and emotional shock rendering him incapacitated, the woman (still in a fighting stance above him) began to talk.

Her parents, she told him, were greatly troubled by all the terrible things that happened in the world, and had taught their daughter martial arts from infancy. If you don't want to be touched, they had schooled her, you must act before it happens. The girl followed her parents' counsel to the letter, and had grown up lashing out at people here, there, and everywhere. It had reached the point now that, whenever she sensed any kind of lascivious intent, her body responded before her mind registered what was happening. Maybe things would have been different if it were someone she really liked, but she'd never really been in love with anybody and wasn't sure what would become of her. Hearing this, the prince finally understood why nowhere on the girl's body had been glowing, and passed out.

Later, he made the decision not to make any rash decisions. To wait things out, and see if the woman got used to him. It would be highly embarrassing if the truth got out—and besides, there was no doubt that this was, indeed, the purest woman in the kingdom. Nobody had ever touched her. She was exactly the kind of woman he wanted. It was common enough, after all, for marriage to be challenging at first. For now, the prince is being beaten up on a daily basis.

English Composition No. 2

"Is that Ophelia over there?"

"No, that's the Lady of Shalott."

"Is that Ophelia over there?"

"Yes, it is."

"Was that person who just went floating by Ophelia?"

"No, that was the Lady of Shalott."

"How do you tell the difference?"

"It's easy. The Lady of Shalott is in a small boat."

"I see. That's easy to understand."

"So this must be the Lady of Shalott?"

"No, this is Ophelia."

"But she appears to be in a small boat."

"Actually, that isn't a boat, but bits of trash. They must have collected around her as she floated downstream."

"Oh, really. I see."

"Look, there by her feet. You can make out a plastic bottle."

"Yes, you're right."

"Is that Ophelia over there?"

"No, that is a homeless person who drowned."

"Hmm, this is really rather difficult."

Dear Doctor Spencer Reid

I am a Japanese high school student, and a huge fan of yours. I first encountered you one day when my mom was watching *Criminal Minds* on the Drama Channel. I was only really watching out of the corner of my eye, until you came on and started solving all kinds of cases. I thought you were so cool.

I'm particularly impressed by your photographic memory. If only I had photographic memory, I'd do so well on my school tests. How amazing that you have an IQ of 187, as well! That's the same IQ as Sheldon in *The Big Bang Theory*. I sometimes wonder why the makers of *The Big Bang Theory* chose the same IQ for Sheldon, even though it came out after *Criminal Minds*. The two characters are totally different, and the series themselves are really dissimilar, so it's a bit confusing. Did you know that when you search "IQ 187" on the internet, yours and Sheldon's photos come up? It's really funny. But a different number like 188 or 186 would have done fine, so I wish they'd gone for that instead. Maybe that's because, as much as I like Sheldon, I much prefer you, and I don't want to have to compare you to anybody.

My mom watches movies and TV series from overseas whenever she can, which means I end up watching them too. Sometimes the shows have girls and boys of my age in them. In the schools in the series set in Asian countries, everyone wears school uniform, so they look like the schools that I know. A lot of Japanese people go around feeling like Japan isn't part of Asia. I once saw a comment on a photo that someone else posted on social media of themselves standing in front of a palm tree by a beach in Atami that read, "It looks like you're in Asia!" Another time I saw someone commenting on photos of someone else's trip to Vietnam, "Ah, wow, Asia looks so cool!" Seeing that, it struck me that they should comment the same thing on photos from Japan: "Ah, wow, Asia looks great!" What need did they have to feel envious when they themselves got to be in Asia every single day? People go on about "trips to Asia," but Japan is *in* Asia, and so holidays in Japan are trips to Asia, too. It's so weird.

Anyway, the schools in America where there's no uniform and everyone gets to wear what they like look so free in comparison. It must be great, not having to wear a school uniform. But you were bullied at school for being clever, so your memories from that time can't be too pleasant. I guess that everywhere's much of a muchness, in the end. Now that you're an adult, though, you're putting all that knowledge to use in solving mysteries. That's really cool.

I sometimes try to imagine what it would be like to be at school in a different country. The me that goes to school in America is called Teresa. Teresa has a best friend called Victoria. The way I imagine it is based on all the things I've seen on TV and in movies so I didn't know if it's at all accurate, but I picture us wandering around the shopping mall together, telling each other about our problems. In reality I don't really have any problems to speak of, so the worries that Teresa and Victoria speak to one another about are things that I've made up. Is that bad? I feel like Teresa is a better listener than she is a talker.

Another version of me goes to school in Thailand. Her name's Mei. She's got really amazing braids. My hair is short, so I have a lot of admiration for people with long hair, which is why I made Mei's hair long. Mei likes going to get food with her friends after school. There are loads of cheap and delicious restaurants and stalls near her house, so it's no problem if Mei's mom doesn't cook her dinner. My mom often says that she's envious of Thai women, not having to cook. Apparently she read that somewhere.

I'm always imagining the various versions of me who live in other places. But I get the feeling that if I was actually living somewhere else, I'd still be imagining other versions of me, in other places. Why is that the place where you find yourself always seems a bit pale and lackluster? I don't like myself all that much, and I always feel kind of disappointed (I don't have a photographic memory, for one thing), and so I end up thinking that the reason the place I'm in seems pale and lackluster is that I'm living here. That would at least provide an explanation. Which is why I end up imagining Teresa and Victoria, and Mei, and so on. This is between you and me, but there's some part of me that believes they actually exist.

What I think about most frequently, though, is you. I think about how you're super-fast at reading, and how kind and sensitive you are, and all the weird things about you, and how, especially at the beginning, you always seemed so awkward, no matter the situation you were in. I just think you're really great.

My dream is to play cards with you someday. I want to play pelmanism with you and watch in rapture as you use your photographic memory to claim all the pairs. I'm going to be your fan forever. I'm going to study really hard so I can get a job in the FBI like you. Tomorrow my end-of-term tests start.

LIFE IS LIKE A BOX OF CHOCOLATES

The different varieties of chocolate, the constituent ingredients, the weight, the possible allergens, the storage instructions, the manufacturer name, the best before date, and various warnings are all written clearly on the box for you, before you open it.

Braids

I was never much of an artist, but I liked drawing braids. Or maybe it was less that I liked drawing them, and more that they were the only thing that I could draw with any degree of competence. As long as I was drawing braids, I could look down and think, yeah, that's not bad. As soon as I started to add in the wildly sparkling eyes and the unnaturally shaped faces that I'd picked up from the shōjo manga that I read, my drawings would begin to flounder. When I went to sketch in bodies, things got even worse. With their arms and legs out of proportion with their heads, and their blouses and skirts unavoidably shabby-looking, the girls I drew were always uncool, in a way not dissimilar to myself, and I hated looking at them. So I stopped drawing anything but braids.

At school, I'd doodle braids in the corner of my notebook during the lessons I found dull. If I drew them in pencil they'd be dark, if I drew them with the yellow highlighter pen I used to underline key points then they'd be blonde, and if I drew them with the red pen I used for marking then it they'd be Anne of Green Gables's braids.

I made the braids longer and longer. Three short lines running down to the right, and next to them, three lines running down to the left: this was the process, repeated ad infinitum. The margins of my textbooks were filled, and when I ran out of space to draw there, the braids would sometimes worm their way into the gaps between the text.

"Urgh, gross," the boy who sat next to me had once remarked.

The blank spaces in his notebook were peopled with badly rendered manga characters. Both of us were unable to listen in lessons without distracting ourselves in some way.

As I went on drawing braids, I began to incorporate objects into them, without fulling intending to. Bows, and daisies, and four-leaf clovers. Cherries, and heart-shaped chocolates. Soon, the bows would end up covered in checks or polka dots, and the cherries would be complete with amoeba-like patches to represent their glassy surfaces. Whatever I incorporated seemed to suit the braids very well.

Over a decade has passed since then, but doodling braids has cemented itself as a habit for me, and I find myself still doing it when I'm bored in meetings or at my desk. They go advancing across my post-it notes and reports.

The same thing is happening right now, in fact. As I argue with my boyfriend on the phone, I'm sketching braids on the back of a flyer with a black Pilot pen. Sometimes you need distractions in order to make it through this world.

As my boyfriend says his piece, and I say mine, the braids keep on growing. It's a pretty big flyer, so there's plenty of space for them to occupy. They twist and turn across the dull pink paper like the squares of a snakes and ladders board, gradually taking over.

The argument is showing no sign of wrapping up. This isn't unusual. We're both quite obstinate people, and our fights tend to drag on.

Wow, this is long, I think to myself as though it were something quite unconnected to me, while I doodle the braids and add in subsidiary objects. Anything will do: a bunch of grapes, a snowflake, a crane, a shooting star, Ursa Minor, the gyoza I ate for dinner. As I draw the gyoza, it strikes me that they actually make great hair accessories. The shape of them isn't unlike some kind of dangly earring.

Then I try scattering the braids with musical symbols—treble clefs, quavers, and so on. Immediately the scene takes on a cheery ambience, the opposite of what's happening on the phone. It's as if the braids are singing.

After a while I return to regular braids, and this time I try adding in something big. I draw in the fridge that I've had ever since I got my own flat, but which finally broke the other day. Then I add braids on top, so that the fridge is soon engulfed.

Sayonara, refrigerator. Thanks for everything.

Next, I attempt a whale. I'm not really sure why. Thanks to all the assorted items I've incorporated into my braids, my drawing skills have improved considerably. I even add in a bunch of little details: a scar on the whale's back, some craggy white bits stuck to its skin. Then the whale is swallowed up by torrents of braids. My braids are powerful. They devour everything, concealing it from view.

"Oh, give me a break," my boyfriend says, so I print the words *Give Me A Break* into the braids.

"I'm sick of this," he says, so that goes in too. *I'm Sick Of This.*

"That should be my line," I reply. It strikes me how funny it would be if he was writing in the words I came out with into braids of his own, though my guess was that he was playing some game on his computer that you could do single-handedly. I'd noticed that he had it bookmarked when I was at his apartment one time.

"The thing about you is you're just always like . . . "

As my boyfriend yammered on and on, I drew his portrait. Unfortunately my people-drawing skills hadn't improved much since childhood. Small eyes, a small mouth. Short hair, a striped shirt and pants. I drew black slip-ons, and wrote in the word VANS. I drew his arms raised in a banzai pose.

"Like the other day when we met and you were like thirty minutes late . . . "

The sound of his irritated voice like background music, I

went on sketching him. Then I sent in the all-powerful hair. As his raised arms were gradually drowned out by waves of braids, it made him look as though he were crying out for help. Eventually even those arms disappeared from view.

Sayonara, boyfriend. Thanks for everything.

The braids went on proliferating, as if the boyfriend hidden beneath them had never existed at all.

"Hey, what's going on?"

So fully absorbed was I by my drawing that I'd forgotten to make any kind of response. Apparently thinking that I'd taken umbrage at something, my boyfriend's tone of voice had grown a little kinder.

"Well look in any case, let's just both be more careful in future, okay?"

"Er, yeah, sure."

When the phone call finally came to an end, I scrunched up the braid-covered flyer that was now all black and bumpy from the pressure of the pen, and tossed it in the trash. The braids vanished from sight. They were just something to keep my hands occupied, nothing more. I headed to the bathroom to heat up the bathwater.

Messing Up the National Anthem

"Wait a minute, what direction does the sun rise in again?"

Dissecting Misogyny

Okay, ladies! Behold this large, newly-sharpened knife with its serrated tip. Isn't it formidable? I've been using it for some years now, and let me tell you, it's my absolute pride and joy.

Right, I'm going to make a start in on the head. This calls for quite a bit of strength—yes, that's right, slicing through a pumpkin seems like child's play in comparison. Not a task for the complete beginner, I assure you, so I wouldn't try this at home. Just take this opportunity to observe, ladies. Accidents can happen all too easily, and I can't accept responsibility for any injuries that occur in the home, I'm afraid.

So you see, I'm applying pressure, like this, to sever the neck. Oof! This is a particularly tough one! I've been doing this for decades now, but from time to time the knife seems to get stuck midway. In this situation, the trick is to bear down on it with your full body weight so it. . . There, see?

Okay, so the head's off. Oh dear, I see one of our audience members is a little distressed. I do understand your feelings entirely, madam, but please try not to shriek, for the sake of the other audience members. Gosh, has that lady over there passed out? Oh, and another one over there? Would someone mind calling an ambulance? Yes, that's it, if you can keep fanning them it would be most helpful. Oh look, this young lady has brought some smelling salts with her. What forethought! I'm impressed. Oh yes, if you don't mind sharing them around, that would be much appreciated. Goodness, what delicate flowers we all are, ladies! I'm mortified to see the distress I've caused. You know I really wouldn't be inflicting this on you if it wasn't necessary, but sometimes sacrifices must be made. This is my job, after all.

So, as the fainters in the house are probably already aware, the head is full of dark, filthy gunk. See the way it's bubbling and gurgling, as if it were spilling out of a sewer or something? It's a peculiar color, isn't it? Very hard to describe, yet uniquely disgusting. Look what it's done to my lab coat! This was spotless when I put it on, and now you can barely see any white for all the splatters. This happens every time. Honestly, it's hard enough just keeping up with the washing in this line of work!

Good, so now I'll move on to the trunk. This is a pretty large specimen, as they go, so it'll take some oomph. As I said before, you really mustn't go trying this at home. These things are definitely best left to professionals like myself.

Okay, so I'm going to open it up, starting from the stomach. This part of the job is hard work, and it's important not to rush it, so I'm taking it one small step at a time. Right, there we are. That's the trunk all opened up now.

Oh, I see we've got a couple more collapsed over there! Maybe it's wise to take a little break at this point. The stench is pretty overpowering, isn't it? You have to wonder what on earth could create a smell as awful as this. In an ideal world, I'd open the windows, but we're tucked away in a windowless corner of the department store . . . There's not a lot I can do. I just ask that you bear it as best you can. We're nearly through, I promise. You know, I've thought for years about a good way of evoking this stench in words, but I still haven't managed to hit on quite the right description. I suppose if I absolutely had to compare it to something, I might say it was a bit like the soles of the Guardian of the Underworld's fungus-infected feet. Or maybe the gelatinous concentrate of a tomato that had been left for decades in the deepest, darkest corner of a rubbish truck until it rotted to a maggot-infested pulp. Of course, I fully appreciate that such simple descriptions can't come close to approximating the nuanced reality of this stink—I'm just saying, if I was *forced* to provide a comparison.

Well, it seems everyone has regained consciousness, so I'll stop nattering on and proceed to the final task, since my allocated time on this demo stage is limited. I appreciate that you ladies all have a lot to do today, too: shopping for groceries, returning home and preparing dinner, and getting through all the other chores that await you. I don't know how many of you heard the announcement a little while ago, but it seems that fresh tuna is on special today in the supermarket on basement level 1.

So, now I'm going to remove the bones. A little piece of trivia for you: the bones are surprisingly flimsy, and come apart right in your hands. If you look carefully, you'll see that there's no core or marrow running through them, and there are whole sections where they aren't even joined together. Look, here! This is a perfect example, see? Oh, this courageous lady is moving her face right up close to have a look.

You see how easy it is to pull them out, though? It seems like a miracle that it ever managed to live in this pathetic state. Sometimes it's hard to even locate the things. Okay, so I'm just going to whisk them out in quick succession . . . It's a breeze, this part! See, I'm all done. A task like this, I'm sure every one of you ladies could manage.

And that concludes my live demonstration! So now you see what misogyny looks like, dissected and slit open. It doesn't make a very pretty sight with its flesh all over the tabletop like that, does it? But we've come to the end now, so there's to be no more fainting, okay ladies?

After you've all sat so patiently through the live dissection, I'm sorry to say that I can't offer you a tasting session. It's just too messy, unfortunately. And as you know better than anyone, the smell is atrocious. It's not really fit for eating, truth be told. I doubt any of you would even want to try.

So, I'm going to just bundle all of this into a black trash bag and throw it away, like this. Another little piece of trivia for you: the remains can be included in the burnable rubbish. They burn very quickly, and turn straight to ash. But no, of course, as previously stated, I don't recommend trying this at home.

So there, it's all gone. Misogyny is no more! Oh, thank you for such generous applause! It's your encouragement that has kept me going all this time. That's no exaggeration. I owe everything to marvelous ladies like you!

Finally, I should tell you that these knives with their astounding cutting potential are just ¥9,800 plus tax for a set of two. That's a special discounted price limited to today only, so I highly recommend seizing this opportunity right now. I will gladly sharpen them for anyone interested, so you can take them home ready to put to use immediately.

Cage in a Cage

Having fallen into the hands of an obsessive fan, Nicholas Cage sat cross-legged in the giant birdcage, an anguished expression written across his face as he pondered what it meant to be loved so intensely that he would be placed in a cage (the fan fed him three lavish meals a day, and continually whispered sweet nothings to him, *I love that broad forehead of yours, I love your eyes welling with pain, I love your steeply arched eyebrows, I love your delivery which makes it impossible to tell whether you're joking or being serious, I love all your interests and hobbies, I love everything about you, I love you so much*, in response to which Cage would tilt his head to the side like a little bird and listen in silence) before finally reaching the conclusion that the kind of love where you needed to imprison the object of your affection in a cage wasn't really love at all, at which point he stood slowly to his feet, blew up the cage, and sped away from the roaring flames on his motorbike.

English Composition No. 3

Do you know Ken? Yes, I know Ken. Where is Ken from? Ken is from Japan. Is Ken tall? Yes, Ken is very tall. Is Ken handsome? Yes, Ken is very handsome. Is Ken wearing trousers? Yes, Ken is wearing trousers. Is Ken wearing a cap? Yes, Ken is wearing a cap. What is Ken's hobby? Ken likes pop music. That is his hobby. Please tell me what kind of pop music Ken likes. Oh, you better ask Ken himself. Where is Ken? Ken lives three blocks away. Take a left at the lights. Does Ken like you? Oh yes, Ken likes me very much. Do you like Ken? Oh yes, I like Ken very much. Do you like the pop music that Ken likes? Oh yes, I like the pop music that Ken likes very much. Is the pop music that Ken likes well known? Oh yes, the pop music that Ken likes is very well known. Does Ken know that the pop music he likes is well known? Yes, Ken knows that the pop music he likes is well known. Do you know that the pop music that Ken likes is well known? Yes, I know that the pop music that Ken likes is well known. That's good to hear. However, John doesn't like the pop music that Ken likes. Who is John? I don't know. Where is Ken now? Ken is in the zoo now. The zoo is three blocks away. Take a left at the lights. I said left, not right. The lights are now red. The sky is blue. What is Ken doing? Ken is looking at the penguins. What is Ken thinking? He is thinking, Don't die, penguins! I don't care if everything else dies, but please save the penguins! Does Ken like penguins? Oh yes, Ken likes penguins very much. Does Ken like pop music and penguins? Oh yes, Ken likes pop music and penguins very much.

The Masculine Touch

The brand-new men's product, which had evolved out of a suggestion made by a male writer that so perfectly exemplified his unique masculine touch, sent shockwaves through Japan. The product was showcased across the internet and in myriad magazines, which were enraptured by how it encapsulated the masculine touch so well, generating a furious buzz as a result and racking up wild sales. Men from all over the country rushed out to buy the product. The person most surprised by the product's riotous success, more rightly termed as a social phenomenon, was the male writer himself.

The more radical of the male novelists wrote articles about this turn of events for male magazines, declaring this the beginning of the Male Era. They bolstered their arguments with examples of the other times when the masculine touch had effected changes like this one, thus arguing for the necessity of men's continued progress into all areas of society.

Hanging from the ceiling of the train carriage, flapping about in the plentiful space up there, an advert for a business magazine featuring an interview with the male writer in question announced in large letters that this was a defining moment for the male perspective. In the bottom right-hand corner of the advert, the male writer stood with his body contorted into an unnatural looking posture, a fawning, doe-eyed expression plastered across his face as he gazed into the camera.

The company's sales force, who had initially frowned and said they weren't at all sure that they bought this masculine touch angle, came to see that maybe it was less of a lost cause than they'd initially thought. Observing those same people who had before looked right through him now making a beeline toward him with a smile that seemed to declare that they'd seen the light, were changed people, the male writer felt stunned by how quickly they'd changed their tune. He had finally been accepted by society.

In actuality, the male writer wasn't a permanent employee of the company that had released the new product. He had participated in an advisory role, as someone with his finger on the pulse of public opinion, and this was his first experience of the world of product development. However, thanks to his unique masculine touch and a dash of beginners luck, the male writer had struck gold.

The male writer's success heralded a multitude of changes in Japanese society. *How does this read in terms of the male perspective, I wonder? Do we not think we might be lacking a masculine touch here? Hold on, should we not get a male opinion on this?* Phrases like these began to fly about in meeting rooms all over Japan. If at least one of these phrases wasn't used over the course of a meeting, then those taking part were beset by anxiety, and when someone cleverly wove one into the conversation, everyone would breathe a sigh of relief.

The attitude of proactively seeking male opinions became fashionable in workplaces nationwide. Those workplaces prioritizing male empowerment used this as a selling point, thereby securing themselves a progressive, forward-thinking image, and ensuring their adoration across society. Sales of products whose names included the word "man" and "male" began to soar. Sales of books written by men went up. Men, in short, were given special treatment, and their masculinity emphasized.

The male writer found himself inundated by requests to

write articles, which had been his main job prior to developing the product, and he was soon a very busy man. His name was splashed all about the media, and he was frequently asked to write reviews of the latest men's films, advice columns for men, and similar. Sometimes, he would take on the slightly more risqué work that he was offered, giving his opinion on male sex toys, or speaking on the question of male desire. He had regular features in men's magazines such as *Man's Own, Men's World,* and *Man and Home* which earned him many accolades. Soon enough, he had become the go-to person when people wanted a male take on something.

Requests also flooded in for lectures and appearances on panels with themes such as *Men's Writing, Careers for Men,* and *Thinking about Men's Rights*. Everyone wanted to hear the male writer's unique male perspective on the various topics impacting men's lives. Feeling that it was his mission to see male power better recognized by society, he accepted every request that came his way. All of his appearances ended with ecstatic applause from the sea of men filling the venue.

During the Q and A sessions at said events, enthusiastic men in the audience would pose questions like "Can you give us your thoughts on what society can do to make it possible for men to stay in employment?", and, "What does the ideal workplace for men look like?", and, "Do you think it's possible for men to keep on working after marriage?" The male writer took seriously every question that he was posed, doing his utmost to answer them as best he could. There were often moments when he would feel overwhelmed by the eager gleam in all these eyes fixed upon him, by the great ambition he sensed in those men. From time to time, he would be so moved that he found himself tearing up.

Not infrequently the male writer would be asked to record a conversation with one or two other working men from other professional fields: a male film director who had just finished shooting a new series featuring a male detective as lead; a male lawyer specializing in male issues; an up-and-coming male architect; the male CEO of a company which had skyrocketed to success. The male writer would converse and exchange opinions with these men who had achieved such dazzling success in their respective areas of expertise, as the male assistants organizing the occasion would look on silently but intently.

The male writer found these opportunities for information exchange very stimulating, personally as well as professionally. After getting home, or in the taxi on the way back, he'd experience a surging sense of unquenchable potency and fulfillment, and took to writing frequently on his blog about his feelings as a man, and his resolve to live his life with grace and flexibility. For the first time in his life, he felt that he wasn't alone—that he was in fact surrounded by like-minded people.

The age of men had arrived. We had come a long way from men finally being granted the vote! The Japanese government enlisted the entire country in supporting men across society. The Prime Minister gave a speech underlining their versatility, and promising, as if by way of setting an example, to include a record number of men in the Cabinet. *Ensuring 30% men in leadership roles!* quickly became a party slogan, and they set about gradually putting this into practice.

The crowning glory in this regard was naturally the appointment of a Minister for Male Empowerment. The newly elected Minister for Male Empowerment spoke passionately of "building a nation where every man can live with pride and confidence, where every man is given the opportunity to flourish," declaring his resolve to "promote new legislation on the participation of men in society." All of this was in service of creating a new world where men could shine.

One day, the male writer received news from his publishing company that a male author, who had once written an essay praising the male writer's achievements, had requested him as his interlocutor in a discussion, which would then be written up for a magazine. The male writer was already a fan of the male author—when it came to writing about men's lives, there was really nobody better—and so he readily agreed. The theme was "What is masculinity?": broad, yet complex. After turning the question over in his mind for a long time, the male writer eventually resolved to wait and see where the conversation on the day took him.

The male writer rode the elevator with its gold surfaces to the top floor of the building. He made his way down a corridor lined with thick carpet to the appointed room. There he found the male author sitting on a couch, talking and laughing with a couple of male editors.

Seeing the male writer, the male author stood up and the two greeted each other. The male author sat down again, and gestured for the male writer to take a seat on the huge leather sofa facing him. Between them lay a hefty glass table holding a selection of the sorts of light snacks favored by men. The male writer felt touched by the thoughtfulness of the male editors. The top floor room was walled in glass, and the windows offered a view of the office district studded with the green of the trees, patches of grass, and parks. In the sky, sunset was approaching and bands of color blended gently.

Soon enough, the discussion commenced. Two voice recorders captured the conversation between the male author and the male writer.

The conversation unfolded so smoothly that it was hard to believe it was the first time the two of them had met.

The male author and the male writer spoke of the various discomforts that came from living as men. They discussed the myriad obstacles lying in the way of male career progression, such as how even when men managed to rise up within the ranks of their workplaces they would inevitably be told that male bosses were hard to work with, and be mocked for being black sheep.

The discussion grew gradually more personal. The male author brought up a particular quote that had rocked him to the core—"one is not born, but becomes a man"—while the male writer talked about how whenever he felt lost in his life as a man, he would bring to mind the line, "In the beginning, man was the sun."

The male author and the male writer spoke eloquently of how the path to our contemporary age, where people came out with things like, "Men are hot right now," and, "This is a man's age," and, "Men are so dynamic," had been paved by the men of the past. They agreed that it was crucial not to let the flame go out—that their mission was to pass on the torch to the men of the future.

The pair's dialogue was at its most lively when they began discussing men as sexual beings. The conversational turn was sparked by a comment that the male author made, saying somewhat forlornly that he didn't understand why he had to be so conscious of himself as a sexual being all the time. Exactly, the male writer said, nodding so fervently it looked as though his neck might snap.

In self-deprecating tones, the male writer and the male author spoke of how tough it was to be a man, of the restrictiveness of being born into a sex where people are constantly demanding manliness from you.

Prefacing his words with the admission that he'd never told anyone this before, the male author spoke of how he'd developed early as a child. He confessed that toward the end of elementary school he'd always been teased about the size of his penis, which had begun to grow before those of the other boys around him. It hadn't stopped growing, either—once he entered middle school, the teasing only escalated.

"His dick is like a D."

"Nah, that's max a C."

"You guys know nothing, that's easily an E."

He described the ridiculousness of being spoken about like this by a bunch of kids who'd only just mastered the Roman alphabet. And yet, even into adulthood, the situation had barely improved.

On TV and in magazines, people would comment constantly on the size of men's penises, and the convenience store magazine sections were threaded with covers featuring pin-up models with huge packages, their hips thrust forward to further accentuate their enormity. What was more, the sizes of the model's lunchboxes increased year on year. The F-size penises that used to cause a stir were now nothing to bat an eye at—it was all about the Hs. More and more people were turning to penis enlargement surgery. How long would this crazy phallomania last?

Reaching the end of his spiel, the male author sighed. As he slurped up the last of his iced tea through his straw, the male writer furiously agreed. He felt exactly the same, he said. It got him down how, wherever you went, all you heard was crass talk about how big or small this or that penis was. Now, spurred on by the male writer's frustrated exclamation that he wished that the other side could experience what it was like to be on the receiving end of everyday sexual harassment, both willful and unconscious, the male author went on.

What makes it worse, he said, is that the lives of everyday men are negatively affected by how the issue is handled on TV. Whenever a man on TV is teased or laughed at for the size of his penis, the male model or male celebrity in question never shows any anger, but merely laughs it off. This attitude had added to the mistaken understanding that male penises were there to be relished and ogled by others.

"Wait a minute, has your dick got smaller?" "Wow, that's a nice cock you've got!" In Japan, where the level of general awareness around sexual harassment was still very low, many men would have comments like these directed casually at them in the workplace. Even if such things weren't said directly to their faces, the dick size of the male employees working there would certainly be discussed amid volleys of laughter:

"He's got cheek acting so tough when he's that small!"

"With a face like that there's no way! I don't care how big it is."

"I'd hit that. Never mind the face."

The male author, who had worked for a spell in an office as a secretary before his debut was published, spoke as someone who had experienced such humiliation first hand. He related regretfully how, in his desperation for his package not to stand out, he had become so self-conscious of his groin area that over time he developed a pigeon-toed way of walking.

Which was why, now that he had established himself as a male author, he felt his role was to instill courage in the men of the world. The penis doesn't belong to them—it's *ours*. Our bodies belong to us. He had begun dressing this way in order to convey that truth. Saying this, the male author proudly indicated his iridescent spandex tights that clung tightly to his genitalia, accentuating their beautiful contours.

Discovering for the first time the reasoning behind the male author's eccentric fashion sense, which was forever being picked apart in the media, the male writer found himself stunned. He felt blood racing hotly around his body, his heartbeat quickening. It wouldn't do, he thought, to keep himself concealed in front of a man like this, who had fought so hard to get where he was.

With a decisive flourish, the male writer stood up from the sofa and deftly unbuckled his belt. His trousers dropped heavily to the floor, like a curtain falling. After taking in the male writer's tights, which revealed a bulge no less beautiful than his own, the male author got to his feet and tore off his shirt with button-ripping momentum.

Grasping immediately what was happening, the male editors moved in smoothly to lift the glass table separating the male author and the male writer and carry it out of the way. The two men in their tights stood locking eyes for a moment, then moved closer. The male editors hurriedly pushed the sofas back to the edge of the room.

Standing at the perfect distance from each other, the male writer and male author clasped hands, elongated their spines, and assumed their poses. A tension filled the room. At that moment, all the men gathered in the space heard the unmistakeable sound of a fanfare.

It was a splendid rendition of the Grand Pas de Deux.

The male author led, with the male writer following one step behind. Pirouette, fouetté, arabesque. Changement, changement, échappé, échappé. Together, the men danced.

When the male author lifted the male writer over his head, the airborne male writer struck a graceful pose. Maintaining this stance, the two paraded around the room, to the sound of the male editors' applause. Unable to contain themselves, the male editors' legs also began to trace the steps.

The male author made numerous leaps through the air, delighting the assembled company with his masculine movements. The male writer contorted his lithe, graceful body alluringly. Drops of sweat flew from the men's bodies. Bathed in the ceiling lights, their tights shone even more fiercely. Releasing the masculinity that they had kept suppressed and pushed down inside themselves for so long, the two men danced with their very hearts and souls. Their male genitalia moved rhythmically in time with their steps. The atmosphere in the room was so rich that every moment seemed to last for an eternity.

Finally, the two reached the coda. The male author's masculine touch and the male writer's masculine touch came together, converged, and fused, creating great undulations in the air. Outside the windows yawned the great night sky. The glass-walled room seemed like a ballroom suspended in the heavens. As the male writer and the male author were leaping and spinning frenziedly at tremendous speed, all the labels reading "man" that had been plastered across their bodies over time—labels that were both a celebration and a curse—began to peel away and fall to the floor. The two forgot their masculinity, and became just two creatures, dancing manically, savoring each other's presence. A sensation that they had never felt before overcame them, as if they were communicating with the universe, and they found themselves letting out cries of unbridled joy.

Sated with elation and delicious exhaustion, the two struck their final poses. There was a moment's silence, and then thunderous applause broke out from across the room. The pair bowed, and smiled. Still standing perfectly still, they basked in the feeling that each and every cell in their bodies had been reborn.

From that day forth, the male writer and the male author went on to scale even greater professional heights, both garnering huge acclaim in their respective fields. Their understanding of the extent to which their maleness had kept them fettered until now enabled both men to enter a new phase of their lives, and they devoted themselves to their work with renewed vigor and drive. No longer held back by anything, they found that their minds were constantly filled with new ideas. This was true gender liberation.

The male writer achieved another hit with a product whose development he'd assisted in an advisory role. This time, an integral part of the product's concept was that it could be enjoyed by anybody, and so the male writer took great pains to avoid any kind of gender specificity. His efforts paid off, and the product sold well. The media once again showered praise on the male writer for his masculine touch.

The male author's latest novel became a bestseller. Its meticulous description of relationships that transcended gender was ecstatically received by the media, who praised its superb masculine touch, and the boldness of its masculine sensibility. The adverts hanging down in the centre of the train carriages proclaimed in large letters: "A fresh and unique masculine touch."

From that point on, everything that the male writer and the male author created, everything that they wrote, was deemed as being the product of their masculine perspective. Everything was put down to their masculine touch.

It's all so fucking stupid.

This thought came, at different places and at different times, to both the male author and the male writer.

Gaban I

No, you mustn't open the jar of maraschino cherries.
That's a specimen jar.
Specimens are made to be looked at.

Gaban II

Red maraschino cherries
Blue maraschino cherries
Yellow maraschino cherries
Green maraschino cherries
Purple maraschino cherries
Brown maraschino cherries
Black maraschino cherries
White maraschino cherries

To You, Sleeping in an Armory

You are asleep, sleep-breathing in your comfortable bed. The moon and stars twinkle in the night sky. The curtains ripple in the breeze. You still haven't realized where it is that you're sleeping. Still haven't realized that you're sleeping in an armory. Your family doesn't realize either.

In the morning, you wake up and sit at the kitchen table. Breakfast is ham and eggs with toast. You munch away. Your mother, washing her face in the sink, still hasn't realized that she's raising a weapon. You drink down the milk she hands you. Your mother is making sure that the weapon gets its calcium.

When you get to school, you greet your friends as you take your place in the classroom. You get out your notebook and pencil case, put them on top of your desk. The homeroom teacher comes in the door. The homeroom teacher still hasn't realized that she's being watched by a stockpile of weapons. That she's about to educate a classroom full of weapons. The students haven't realized either, that they themselves are weapons.

At break time, you race outside with your friends to the playground. You dribble the ball gleefully. You throw the ball gleefully. You jump rope gleefully. You play tag gleefully. You and your friends don't know that wherever you are, that place becomes an armory. The bell rings, and you all go back to the classroom, so now the classroom becomes an armory. While you're making your way to the art room, the corridor becomes an armory.

When you leave school, your route home becomes an armory.

Desperate for your dinner, you dash over the crossroads. Your mom told you that morning that tonight it would be curry for dinner. In the past, any number of you had gone running across this same crossroads, hearts racing at the thought of curry. The cushioning in your sneakers gives you bounce.

After dinner, you get in the bath with your brother, and wash each other's backs. Your brother hasn't realized that he's washing a weapon.

You fall exhausted into sleep. Lying there in the armory, you are dreaming. You dream you're in a fairytale kingdom. You still haven't realized that even when you're dreaming, you're in an armory. Your family, the townspeople haven't realized, that the town in which you live has become an armory. That they themselves are weapons.

A quiet night. The dewdrops go slipping across the leaves. Everyone is sleeping soundly.

CV

Birthplace: Okayama

Highest Educational Qualification: BA in Japanese Literature

Licenses and Certificates: Secretarial Diploma, Level 2; Practical English Proficiency Test, Level 2; Driving License (automatic transmission only).

Professional Experience:

Age 22. Worked as a secretary for ____ University. Tasks included photocopying, serving tea, and carrying out various odd jobs for the professors.

All the academics were men. As I navigated my way through that huge, labyrinthine university building, turning corner after corner, ascending and descending the spiral staircases, I would catch sight of men in white lab coats, peering curiously at me through the plumes of strange-colored vapor rising from the beakers they clasped in their hands.

I began receiving strange emails from a man at work with whom I'd barely exchanged a word. When I didn't reply for a couple of days, a follow-up email arrived saying, *Why haven't you replied? I feel as though I'm going out of my mind.* You're already out of your mind, I thought. In the end a vengeful letter written in brush pen arrived at my house. My mother was terrified. All of the women I met subsequently who had worked in institutions consisting mostly of men had eventually quit after being stalked. Nearly every single one of them.

When, upon tendering my resignation, I informed the university of my intention to use up my paid leave, a professor on a salary several dozens of times greater than mine said, "Don't you think it's a bit odd to pay you for the days you haven't worked? If we don't need to pay you, then we probably won't." With that, he put in a call to the accounts department. After putting down the receiver, he said, "Well, it seems there's a rule that you can. So, fine." His tone was free of compunction. A vision of the elderly woman in the accounts department explaining the matter impassively rose to my mind. The professor in his fifties was seemingly very intelligent, and must have employed many secretaries in his time, and yet he didn't know that the "girls" in the same room as him who looked after his "odd jobs" for him were entitled to receive paid leave.

Resigned for personal reasons.

Age 25. Registered with ____ temp agency.

I was referred to a receptionist role at ____. I sat behind the reception desk in the lobby in a line of other receptionists, all dressed in an identical uniform and smiling.

The uniform was a tight beige two-piece suit (skirt, not trousers, of course), which was a pain when you were on your period. Actually, it was a pain even when you weren't on your period, and so were the tights. Male employees wearing creased shirts and ill-fitting suits would say to me, "You've not got much make up on today, have you?" or, "Have you had a haircut? It looked better before." That, too, was a pain.

There was a largeish hole in the lobby, and occasionally people would fall in and die. The bottom of the hole was so deep that you couldn't see it. Us girls at the reception desk would talk about how they should fill it in, but apparently it wasn't as simple as all that. I said the same thing to a male employee of the company, who I wound up dating, but he would just laugh and pat my head, saying, "A girl like you wouldn't understand," and, "It's not something you need to worry your pretty little head about."

Like a row of dolls we sat there, day in and day out. When moss started to grow on my body, the other girls looked concerned, saying, hey, you better watch out. I could see that my time was approaching. One day, the reception girl who'd been there the longest turned into a stone statue of a boddhisatva. Unable to move of her own volition, she was carried by the security guards into the changing room. That stone boddhisatva sat there in the corner of the changing room, watching over us. We'd change over its bib from season to season, and leave it offerings of snacks.

Resigned for personal reasons.

Age 28. Worked as a domestic help.

Age 29. Administrative role at ____ corporation.

The company had a mysterious room known as the Time Room. The people who went in there wouldn't emerge for years, and were treated as if they'd been posted overseas.

As an enjoyable diversion, the male employees would stop by the female admin section for a chat. They didn't approach the permanent employees, whose apparent busyness rendered them "unapproachable," but they seemed to think those on a temporary contract would be an easier target, and more likely to listen to what they had to say. They saw nothing remotely problematic about repeatedly interrupting people's work.

The only thing that I really accumulated while I was there were memories of being treated as "a woman," as "a girl." These memories piled up, and there were times when everything else seemed to crumble away. It was as if my job in fact had nothing to do with the mound of documents in front of me, but rather consisted of behaving as "a woman", or as "a girl," and being treated in that way. And what a tedious job that was.

Resigned for personal reasons.

Age 32. About to have an interview for a new job.

I pick up the receiver of the phone in the entrance to the office, and punch in the extension number I've been given. The rendition of John Lennon's "Imagine" that plays as the ringtone makes me want to turn around and go home immediately. I've been in the job market for ten years, but I don't feel as though I've ever had an actual job. There's so much I don't get about the world of work. I'm guessing that the next decade is going to be just as much of a headfuck.

Baseball Player Soup

When I woke up, the house was quiet. I poked my head into the kitchen, but my mom was nowhere to be seen. Remembering that today was the day my aunt was supposed to come over, I figured my mom must have had my dad drive her to the supermarket.

I took out a can of soup with a red and white label from the cupboard, shook it vigorously up and down, then poured its contents into a small pan. I added in some milk from the fridge and, when it had warmed, shook in some macaroni from the box.

Sitting on a chair with one knee propped up, I ate the macaroni soup I'd poured into a cafe au lait bowl. It was Sunday, and I was still in my pajamas.

Bits of macaroni bobbed around in the creamy soup. The orange of the carrots, the brown of the mushrooms—the other colors provided an unobtrusive accompaniment. The starring role was reserved for the macaroni, which had absorbed all the water in the soup and were fit to burst.

I put a piece of macaroni in my mouth and chewed and chewed and chewed and chewed. It was a good texture, this. Chewing and chewing and chewing and chewing, I felt as though I was on the cusp of having some sort of insight.

What, though? I stirred my soup as I wondered. The ridged macaroni cylinders swirled round and round, popping up here and there above the surface. As I watched the contents of my soup bowl circulating, it suddenly came to me.

Baseball players. Those plump macaroni looked a hell of a lot like the well-rounded thighs of baseball players. The grooves etched into the macaroni were the stripes on their kit. Inside the bowl of soup, the endless legs of the baseball players intertwined. They sank down only to rise back up again, showing off their succulent shapes.

I licked my lips. I chased down one of those legs trying its best to evade me, then raised the spoon to my mouth. With each mouthful I chewed and chewed and chewed and chewed, appreciatively. One after another, I slurped up and savored the legs of the baseball players who hadn't been quick enough to evade my spoon. Delicious soup seeped out of those muscular thighs. Above the thighs were firm buttocks. The thought made me feel like I was doing something a bit transgressive. Maybe my overactive imagination was a sign that I was tired. Work had been busy lately, after all. But there was no sin in just imagining things, surely? With a wry smile, I polished off what was left of the macaroni. When I was done eating, I said to myself, I'd better get to cleaning my room.

Just then, my aunt came into the kitchen, wheeling a suitcase.

"The front door was unlocked! You shouldn't leave it like that, you know, it's dangerous. Oh! Where're your mom and dad?"

My aunt, my beloved aunt. I hadn't seen her in a long time. I smiled, opening my mouth wide. Before I knew it, my aunt was screaming. From her position on the floor, where she'd collapsed in shock, she croaked,

"Your mouth! Your mouth's bright red!"

I went on smiling, ever wider. I could feel the baseball players' blood dribbling down from the sides of my mouth.

Curtain of Celebration

The curtain fluttering and flapping in the corner of the classroom was the same color as my school uniform shirt. As I watched that scrap of wavering white, I found myself succumbing to its hypnotic power, growing progressively more sleepy. I didn't need to look around the classroom to know that there were many others in the exact same predicament. It was always this way in the afternoon.

How much more exciting things would be with a curtain of a brighter shade! Thinking this, I recalled the multicolored curtain that existed overseas. An extraordinarily big curtain that filled the entire sky. It fluttered over the heads of the people who lived there, its beautiful bright colors shifting. It was almost as if it were celebrating the people living there, celebrating their lives.

I began to feel envious of those people. I wanted to experience what it was like to have my life celebrated daily by some huge, beautiful entity suspended in the sky. I guessed that at first it would feel quite overwhelming, may take a moment to get used to. But after a while, it would become commonplace. How special was that?

People who'd never been to the place where the curtain was could find images and videos online that provided a sense of what it was like, but they couldn't convey how amazing the experience was. It was almost bizarre the extent to which they failed to convey its reality. Whenever I encountered them, they didn't give you the feeling of having been there, having seen the curtain.

Half-listening to the teacher's voice, I looked outside the window. No clouds in the sky today. I was still unable to travel far away from here, as I longed to. All I had was the boring, dust-covered white curtain. It was so unfair.

If only it was far, far bigger—finding myself thinking this quite seriously, I smiled inwardly. If only the curtain over the sea was so vast, so long, that it extended above all of our heads too. If only it were big enough that it incorporated every single person on earth. Then we could all live out our lives being celebrated, constantly.

Of course I knew that that was impossible. That was exactly why I tried to imagine it—why I imagined that the white curtain in front of me was inextricably connected to the brightly colored one. Why I imagined that big curtain in a far-off country was celebrating us. That it hadn't forgotten about us.

I decided, then and there, to act as if that were the case. I resolved to believe that I was being celebrated at every possible moment—when I was writing in my notebook with my pencil, when I picked up the ruler I'd dropped, when I was walking through the covered passageway to the next lesson. Right now, this very instant. That was how I would live my life, until the day that I could see that curtain of celebration with my own eyes. Until I could say, thanks for everything, and celebrate the existence of that curtain in turn.

Remembering Technology

Your first ever technology tastes just like melon soda. It's the exact same luminous green as the melon soda that is dispensed by those technological devices. A shade that barely seems real, like the neon-colored emeralds on the flyers for the jewelry stores my mom used to look at. When I bring the cup up to my mouth, technology crackles as it jumps up beneath my nose. I put technology to my lips. Technology fizzes and flies in my mouth. I reel with delight at how it tastes. The flavor barely seems real. The smell barely seems real. With my teeth, I crunch the bits of ice that have been crushed into identical shapes by a technological device. If I don't finish it quickly, the paper cup will grow floppy. The outside of the cup is already soaked with condensation. Hurriedly I drink the technology down. I feel the power of technology welling up inside me, filling my entire body.

Technology pops and bursts. Technology is a beautiful color. It's always like that. I tilt my head up and shake the small bag above my open lips, and technology snaps and jumps inside my mouth like fireworks. I use the magic wand of technology to refine technology, over and over again, like the witches on TV showed me how. When you refine technology, it changes color. It changes taste. It tastes even better. With a big grin on my face, I lick technology from a plastic spoon. I pour water onto technology, and a stream of tiny bubbles goes rising up, then technology comes cascading out of the cup in all its lurid glory. Technology dyes our tongues in an instant, and makes them go numb. We poke out our tongues at each other, examining their new strange colors, then cackle with insane laughter. Technology inflates. Technology sets. Technology dissolves. Technology glows. Technology flows. Technology festers. Technology knows no limits. Technology bewitches like magic does.

For as long as we can remember, we have been obsessed with technology. We adore it. After all, we are the children of science! We always will be, however old we get. Just imagining a life without technology makes us want to die of boredom. An existence like that is unthinkable. We remember technology fondly. We think back to the various things with which we used to share our lives that have since disappeared, and we feel a sense of nostalgia. We love the new bits of technology that appear before us unconditionally. We are good friends with technology. The bonds that tie us are ever so strong. Way, way stronger than those we have with history or whatever. And they say we've descended from apes! From those shaggy old things! That we used to live in caves! Please! All that stuff has no relation to us. It's just stuff you learn in social studies class. Just stuff to fill in on tests. With the pencils that technology has bestowed upon us—mechanical pencils! Remember those rocket pencils, with all those little lead sections whose order you could change around? They were the product of technology too. Though of course, those rockets couldn't actually fly. Unfortunately.

We couldn't give a toss about history and past ages and all that tedious nonsense. We really don't feel there's any need to "take the broader view" with any of this stuff. You can leave that crap to the guys with too much time on their hands as far as we're concerned. We're going to live the lives we want. We want to really *feel* technology—with our own eyes, with our own minds. Our very own technology. The technology that brings a twinkle to our eyes like nothing else. Then it will become part of our memories. Our most precious memories.

Even as we speak, we're walking around with technology in our hands. We listen to technology as we smell technology. We get on technology, and enter technology. We choose the very best technology. The technology we choose is so slick it makes us swoon. We show off our technology. We boast about it. We size it up. We stamp our feet in frustrated envy at our friends' technology. We compete with our technology. Bang! Crash! Boom! Our technology explodes. We use our technology to start over, overwrite what was there before. We plead with our technology: *Make me win, make me win, make me win, make me win.* Our lives are made of technology.

We walk alongside technology, we delight in technology, we grieve over technology, we are saved by technology, we bemoan technology's limits, we feel gratitude for technology's power, we lie down surrounded by technology, and close our eyes for eternity. We are chosen by technology. Technology burns our bodies, buries us in the earth, then quickly moves on. Technology is busy. Technology doesn't have time to look back to the past. Technology has no need for our memories.

Bird Strike!

If humans were going to go ahead and develop engines that couldn't be damaged by birds, that left birds with no choice but to develop birds that couldn't be damaged by engines. Birds that wouldn't be sucked up into engines and pulverized like mincemeat. Just how many birds had been sacrificed that way? Enough was enough. What birds needed was the power of steel, and bodies of a size that couldn't fly into engines, even in error.

It's hard to distinguish avian airplanes from regular airplanes. That's because they're not made in an amateurish way—unlike that bus that you can tell is a cat from a mile away, for instance. Even once you're inside, the experience is comparable to being in a real airplane. The birds have been careful enough to distinguish between first and economy class. They have the glossy catalogues of duty free goods. They have the itchy blankets. The selection of movies and music, old and new. The smooth landings. The birds assure humans a comfortable trip through the skies. The birds take pride in excelling over humans.

Not even the engineers, let alone the pilots and cabin attendants, have ever harbored any suspicions. It's totally unthinkable, of course, that the perfect avian airplanes would have any faults, but to escape suspicion from humans they make sure to have the odd screw coming loose and the odd engine going awry from time to time. They have to meet humans on their level. The engineers repair the birds, and the birds readily accept their repairs. Very occasionally, a child will find a feather beneath one of the seats and show it to their mothers, saying *Mommy, look*, but the birds don't see that as any kind of failing.

The National Anthem Goes to New York

Where East 29th Street intersects with Madison Avenue, the National Anthem saw two young men holding hands. In slim-fitting pants and T-shirts, the slender young men looked very happy. Their step, as they walked along in their sneakers, was light, and they were smiling as they made their way past the National Anthem. Their white teeth sparkled, their eyes sparkled, their blonde and brown heads of hair sparkled, the glasses that one of them was wearing sparkled, the two of them were sparkling. It was the first time for the National Anthem to see people radiating love in that way. For the first time, the National Anthem understood the abstract concept of love as a tangible, concrete reality. There were couples everywhere, and the National Anthem had seen lots of them, but this kind of couple was new. What a beautiful thing love is, the National Anthem thought, and began to cry.

[An extract from the National Anthem's diary from that day.]

. . . I honestly thought that I was done with love, because it was just too painful, but seeing that pair sparkling in that way, I felt my feelings start to sparkle as well, and that enabled me to feel more hopeful about falling in love again myself. It's cheered me up so much, seeing that. I feel as though being in that exact place at that exact moment was a piece of great luck. In fact, I can't help but feel like I came to New York specifically in order to see that couple. There are loads of psychic shops here, which

is kind of fun. Seeing their neon signs in all those spooky colors is really exciting to me. I wonder how many of the mediums in this city can see me. I guess that if I suddenly walked into one of the shops, they'd get a surprise. The fossils that I saw today in the American Museum of Natural History were very . . .

Flora

Mei sat leaning against her bedroom wall, flipping through a book of pre-Raphaelite paintings. The cold plaster wall felt good through her white school uniform shirt, and she could hear all kinds of noise coming from outside the window. Her uncle had brought the big, heavy book back for her from his trip to the UK. He seemed to have remembered that Mei was in art club at school. The boxes of tea and biscuits he'd also brought back with him were now sitting on the shelves in the living room. Both boxes were very pretty, and Mei's mom had been delighted by them.

When Mei moved her bare feet, the shiny silk bedspread slid a little. Mei had wanted one with Sanrio characters on it, but her mom had objected. Ignoring the slipping and shifting of the bedspread, she went on turning the stiff pages of the book. One of the distinctive features about pre-Raphaelite art was the attention paid to rendering nature, as well as people. Great care had gone into depicting small flowers and plants, without any simplification, which made them endlessly fascinating to look at.

Mei was particularly fond of a picture by Evelyn de Morgan called *Flora*. In the paintings by the other artists, the meticulously depicted plants were always perfectly balanced, which signaled to Mei that the artists were clear on what the focus of the paintings really was. The people were the main act, regardless of how intricately the plants were rendered. That was how the human gaze worked—faced with people and objects, it could tell, just by looking, which was the most important.

The same was true among people, in fact. Faced with man, a woman, and a child, a lot of people would act as though the order of importance was self-evidently man > woman > child. Mei was at the bottom of this hierarchy, so she understood immediately when this was happening. She guessed that people at the top of the hierarchy didn't really get that. It was funny to her that those people acted so superior, when there was this thing that everyone else understood and they didn't.

And yet in *Flora*, the Evelyn de Morgan painting, the plants seemed just as full of life as the person. Both of them looked completely alive. The painting showed a woman with long golden hair, a spread of wild flowers at her feet. The flowers didn't seem any lesser than her, and neither did they seem as though they were being trodden on. They were being trodden on, of course, but they weren't *really* being trodden on. Mei suspected that the person who'd painted this viewed people and plants as equally important. That was a pretty amazing thought. Mei wanted to try seeing the world through Evelyn de Morgan's eyes. Things must have looked considerably different through them, she thought. Although maybe now that Mei had seen the world as de Morgan saw it, via her painting, things would look different to her, too. That was an incredible idea.

Mei's mom appeared at the door that Mei had left open.

"Will you go and get a few bits for dinner? Anything you like."

"Sure."

Mei didn't mind being sent out to the food stalls. Today, she decided, she'd buy a selection of her all-time favorite things. Internally she pumped her fists in the air.

Shutting the book, Mei got to her feet. She took the money from her mother, put on her sandals, and headed out into the world with a new set of eyes.

Twenty-First Century Tinkerbell

A clear blue day, and the afternoon sun slipped effortlessly through the line of unsuspecting trees, emerging the other side not as dappled light but a full, unadulterated stream. Its brightness made Tinkerbell wince. Her tiny body wavered as she was set off balance, and she hurriedly flew toward the nearest object.

But wait—this object was smooth. Slippery, even.

Tinkerbell's landing pad turned out to be the hair of a woman walking down the street. Realizing that it would have been all too easy to slide all the way down to the bottom of her shoulder-length caramel locks and away, Tinkerbell clung on tightly.

The woman strode ahead with unerring footsteps. When her shoulders moved, Tinkerbell moved also. It was as though she'd become a Christmas tree decoration. The thought was amusing to her. As she rocked from side to side, Tinkerbell risked a glance at the woman's profile. Eyelashes curled firmly upward, lips painted a plum shade. The glittery highlighter along her cheekbones sparkled in the light. Tinkerbell kicked playfully at the woman's dangly silver earrings that were swaying about just like she was.

A noise began sounding from the pocket of the woman's jeans. The woman took out her smartphone and raised it to her ear, beginning to talk without reducing her walking speed. (Even Tinkerbell knew about smartphones. She was, after all, the twenty-first century Tinkerbell.)

"Oh, hi! It's been ages. Yeah, I'm good. You?"

A self-possessed, direct sort of voice, surpassing the lively domain and entering hearty territory. Tinkerbell liked the woman's voice.

From where Tinkerbell was stationed, she could hear, too, the voice of the person that the woman was talking to. She understood, from what the faceless person was saying, that the woman's name was Nico. Quite possibly it was a nickname. The voice without a face was asking what Nico's plans were for the day ahead.

"I'm doing an all-night movie soirée with a few friends in a hotel room. Each of us brings along our favorite DVDs and a bunch of snacks. There're hotels that offer that kind of plan for a reasonable rate. There's an LCD screen, and they've even got karaoke, apparently."

After giving this cheery reply, Nico said goodbye, ended the call and crossed the street at the pedestrian crossing.

For a second, Tinkerbell's thoughts turned to Peter Pan. Hadn't someone said he'd gone off the rails? Tinkerbell's gaze roved around her for a while, but she then snapped back to herself. Actually, she thought, this seemed like way more fun.

Dangling just above Nico's ear, full of excited expectation, Tinkerbell made her whole body glow.

The Start of the Weekend

I bought a 124 yen and a 365 yen in the convenience store and went back to my 64,000 yen. I changed into a 1,990 yen, and ate the 124 yen and the 365 yen on a 7,190 yen. I put 330 yen on the 190 yen and brushed, washed my face with a 371 yen, and wiped with a 500 yen. I sank down onto the 1,980 yen placed on the 16,800 yen, lay my head on the 999 yen in the 1017 yen, and put the 5,500 yen over me. I'd been doing a lot of overtime of late, so I fell immediately into sleep and had a good 0 yen. Midway through, though, it turned into a bad 0 yen, and I clung tightly to the 5,500 yen.

Reflection

I spotted someone who may have been the protagonist, but the glare prevented me from getting a proper look. A figure seemed to be heading in that direction, but they were in my blind spot. I couldn't see the criminal because the light was too bright and made me squint. I felt like I'd registered the color of their clothing, but perception of color is a subjective thing, and I can't be sure I got it right. The photo I took at the time was into the sun and came out all blurry. The object that held the key to the whole case lay at the bottom of the swimming pool, but it was obscured by the ripples on the water. I wanted to write down all kinds of pertinent facts in my notepad, but my pencil was too short. Some of the characters appeared on the verge of discussing something important, but a nearby car sounded its horn at just that moment, and I couldn't make out what was said. I turned my head to look in that direction and missed out on seeing the weapon. Just as the victim's relatives were about to talk about the terrible curse passed down through their family for generations, someone put headphones on me from behind, so I couldn't hear what they said. That came as a surprise. Inside the mansion the criminals were beating up the main characters one after another, but the door was locked so I couldn't get in. I tried to peer in through the window, but I wasn't tall enough. I dragged a big rock over to the window and tried to climb on top of it, but just then someone inside closed the curtains. I tried holding a paper cup to the window and pressing my ear to it, but suddenly all fell silent.

The story ran away from me.

When the Girl Broke Up with Her Boyfriend

When the girl broke up with her boyfriend, her mother was pleased. The man was an idiot, a fool, her mother said. The girl agreed. When the girl found a new boyfriend, her mother was pleased. It's good to have a man to count on, he'll help you out, her mother said. The girl agreed. When the girl broke up with her boyfriend, her mother was pleased. The man was a good-for-nothing, the cheating type, her mother said. The girl agreed. When the girl found a new boyfriend, her mother was pleased. It's hard for a woman to live alone, it's good to have some support, her mother said. The girl agreed. When the girl broke up with her boyfriend, her mother was pleased. He was self-righteous and selfish, her mother said. The girl agreed. When the girl found a new boyfriend, her mother was pleased. It's not good for a person to always get their own way, it's important to learn to compromise, her mother said. The girl agreed. When the girl broke up with her boyfriend, her mother was pleased. My daughter is not a maid, it's a relief that she's rid of a man like that, her mother said. The girl agreed. Every time the girl broke up with her boyfriend, her mother was pleased, and every time the girl found a boyfriend her mother was pleased. I watched it happen, time and time again.

A Father and His Back

A *child grows up watching his father's back*, goes the old adage, but this particular father didn't want his son watching his back. The father felt a lot of pressure at the idea of being observed like that, and the notion that the orientation of his own back might be driving his son in a certain direction seemed too heavy a burden to bear. He didn't want his back communicating things to his son that he wasn't aware of.

The son grew into a healthy young boy, and the father took meticulous care not to show his back to him. Hiding his back from a baby had been simple enough, but once the boy started walking, the father had to respond to his son's movements, constantly turning this way or that to evade his gaze. He became very adept at walking backwards and sideways. The sight of his father doing all this was so amusing that it often had the boy in stitches.

At home, the father took up position at the side of the room wherever possible, spending all his time with his back pressed flat against the walls. In their household, the idea of father and son taking a bath together and scrubbing each other's backs was entirely out of the question.

In primary school the boy made a clay model of his father that was just like one of Giacometti's cat or dog sculptures. Giacometti never properly observed a cat or dog except head-on, so his sculptures of these creatures have heads that are fully fleshed out, while the rest of their bodies are thin as wire. On a middle-school excursion to a dilapidated old theme park, the boy saw a row of panels designed to look like a street of houses from some foreign country. The fronts of the panels had been painted with illustrations of colorful houses, but their backs were just the exposed wooden frames holding them up. Asked about them upon returning home, the boy commented, "They were just like Dad." Whenever the boy saw crabs, he was reminded of his father. When the boy encountered the nurikabe, a spirit that manifests as a plaster wall and blocks passers-by, he was reminded of his father.

The father was perpetually on the run from his son, inwardly entreating the boy not to look at his back, and doing everything he could to avoid showing it to him, and yet relations between the two were not particularly bad. In fact, it was only when the father was hugging his son that he was freed from the worry of having his back seen by him, and so the boy grew up being constantly embraced by his father.

The Beginning

There's a flower whose meaning is "youth and sadness," a phrase of which I felt much fonder than I did of the flower associated with it. I discovered it on a black-and-white page of a otherwise colorful book, a page that wouldn't have stuck with me at all if I hadn't happened to notice those particular words beneath the photograph. Looking up the flower in an illustrated guide, I found it to be a smug-looking sort in pale pink and white, whose appearance didn't really match up with its meaning. I kept a hold of its meaning, nevertheless.

Phase One

At the time I first stumbled upon the words in question I was young—sufficiently young enough that youth wasn't something I needed to think about. The same went for sadness. Still, upon discovering that phrase *youth and sadness*, I began thinking about youth and sadness all the time.

When I split up with my first boyfriend after two months, I thought to myself: this must be youth and sadness. In truth, I didn't really feel all that much about the break-up, but it seemed to me nonetheless that there was nothing else that this could be. Break-ups were sad by definition, and I was young.

The first time I had sex, the words ran through my head with every tremor that passed through my body: *youth and sadness, youth and sadness, youth and sadness . . .*

When I messed up at my part-time job as a waitress and the floor manager told me off, I would think to myself that maybe this, too, was youth and sadness. In truth, the sense of vexation I felt toward that horrible floor manager outweighed any sadness I felt, but I thought it still counted. It wasn't youth and happiness, that was for sure.

But then it struck me that actually, the times that were closer to youth and sadness were those occasions when there were no customers and I would hold my tray to my chest, staring down at the floor aimlessly only to catch sight of the tights I'd bought in bulk in the hundred-yen shop and my cheap shoes with numerous white scratches on them.

Phase Two

Now that my eyes had been opened to youth and sadness, I was in no doubt of its existence. It was there amid all the things that happened in my daily life. If I hadn't had the use of this phrase, how would I have described such things? I wondered. Maybe without these particular words at hand, I'd have been less conscious of youth and sadness in my life. Would that have made things easier?

But that wasn't a big problem for me. There were still many times when I didn't realize that what was going on was youth and sadness.

The teacher never once complimented my body. As he stroked my arms, chest, legs, he never told me how beautiful they were. And so I believed my body wasn't beautiful. I had always believed that, but I came to believe it more strongly. The teacher knew that I was beautiful in my youth, and not just in terms of my appearance, and yet he hid it from me. If he'd told me, then I'd have known how beautiful I was. He should have told me. And yet, I didn't realize at the time that this was youth and sadness. I felt that it was the joy of being chosen. It was only as it became clear that the same thing was happening to several of the students that I knew. Did he know that he was adding to the amount of youth and sadness in this world?

Sometimes it took time to notice that something was youth and sadness.

Phase Three

Even once I was a bit older, I was still young. Youth and sadness still followed me around.

I keyed in the extension number I'd been given. The phone ringtone was "Beautiful Dreamer." This was, without doubt, youth and sadness. Such were my thoughts as I responded to the interviewer's questions. "Beautiful Dreamer," the badly fitting suit, and the essay on *My Morning Routine* that I was for some reason made to write—this was all youth and sadness.

Every morning, when I glimpsed my pale face in the mirror above the sink, I would think to myself, youth and sadness. I myself was youth and sadness, and youth and sadness was me.

After the Final Phase

These days, I don't look in the mirror and think, youth and sadness. As my face accumulated wrinkles and lost its former tautness, I was freed, little by little. Then the end came, a bit like the menopause: I was severed from youth and sadness entirely.

And yet, all over the city, I catch glimpses of it. In an empty train carriage at night, a girl in an interview suit is slumped against the door, gazing out the window. Seeing her blank face reflected in the glass, I think to myself, youth and sadness.

Sitting at Starbucks a table along from a young couple looking at each other with bored looking faces I think, youth and sadness.

At the supermarket register, a young man is packing groceries into bags with an unpracticed air. Worrying about the deli items he's put in at an angle, I think to myself, youth and sadness.

Conclusion

Who was it that said that youth is the best time of a person's life, the time that a person shines the brightest? If those really were our days of glory, then none of the adults around us had gotten the memo. They treated us as if we were less than them. Quaking with the anxiety and the sense of inferiority that the adults had planted in me, my body got old, my mind got old, and then my youth was over. My youth was sad. And I never had any money.

Bette Davis

The group sitting round the circular table wearing tense looks on their faces joined their hands. Finding the touch of one another's dry palms a great comfort, they awaited the crucial moment. At one point they thought that they heard a rumble of thunder from outside the window, but it turned out just to be Nakamura's message tone. He said that he liked it because it added a welcome injection of drama into the boredom of his daily life when it went off during his commute and so on. He encouraged us all to try it, and experience the sense of excited anticipation it generated.

The medium was sitting between Kobayashi and Hirata. We'd played rock-paper-scissors beforehand to determine our positions around the table, so that there wouldn't be any embarrassing scramble for places in front of the medium. Saitō, who had dropped out of the rock-paper-scissors game first, still looked a bit disappointed.

We'd flown the medium over from New York for the occasion. She hadn't been cheap, but nobody had any regrets. Sano, who was knowledgeable about all this stuff, had done the research, carefully scouring the reviews and so on before giving her his seal of approval.

Convinced that everything had to be just right, Hirata had taken the day off work so as to pick the medium up at the airport. The messages that she sent on our group chat—which she'd apparently written while the medium was in the airport toilet—read: *The psychic's wearing jeans. Do you think that's okay? I'm a bit worried.* This had unnerved the rest of us, who were at our respective workplaces at the time, and we'd sent a range of concerned emojis. To add to our anxiety, Hirata sent a follow-up message: *And her suitcase is a brand-new Rimowa. I was imagining some kind of woven tapestry bag, or a battered leather thing.* But the one-liner from Kobayashi, the most senior in the group, reading *Her clothes can't tell us anything about her abilities* calmed us down.

Hirata drove the medium to the hotel, where she would rest for a while before Hirata returned to pick her up in the evening. Hirata was secretly very relieved to see that when she reappeared, she had changed into a more medium-like outfit: a black dress with over-long sleeves and hem, together with a wreath of long, beaded necklaces. When the medium arrived at Sano's house, a look of joy spread over everyone's faces.

"Is that really it?" Such was the medium's reaction when we sat down together in Sano's living room and told her what we wanted her to do.

We took a moment to pose ourselves this question. There were many other things we could have asked for. Kobayashi's brother, from whom he'd been estranged for many years, had passed away the previous summer, and he deeply regretted that the last time they'd spoken had been a stupid argument. Nakamura, meanwhile, had wanted for a long time to know the meaning of his grandmother's final words to him. But today wasn't the day for any of these requests. As we all looked at one another and nodded, seriously, a look of incredulity passed over the medium's face.

We gathered around the table, joined hands, and shut our eyes. The flames of the large number of candles placed on the table flickered on the reverse of our eyelids. The medium opened her mouth solemnly.

"Bette, are you there? Come to us from the spirit world."

Someone swallowed audibly. We gripped each other's hands

tighter. The medium went on. We all felt that the curtains were flapping more vigorously than before.

"Bette, Bette Davis. I have some people here who want to speak with you. Come to us, Bette!"

At that moment, we could tell that the medium's head had dropped forward heavily. Everyone's chests began to flutter at this most expected of developments. Sensing the medium lift up her head again—though the truth was that everyone had their eyes opened a crack already, determined not to miss a thing—we all opened our eyes timidly. The expression on the medium's face was that strong, dignified expression that had graced the silver screen.

"What!? Who are y'all?"

We all knew that low, sarcastic drawl well. Plucking up the courage, Nakamura spoke. "Are you really Bette Davis?"

The medium cocked her head, shooting Nakamura a saucy glance as she answered, "That I am, but what the hell do you want? My champagne's gonna get warm at this rate."

It was Bette Davis! Bette Davis was really here! A cheer went up from the group.

"We're huge fans of yours."

"Is it over familiar to call you Bette?"

"I love you, Bette!"

We forgot ourselves, pouring out our true feelings to her.

Bette answered each of us in turn: "Say, isn't that nice!"

"That's just fine."

"Well, thank you very much."

She didn't seem too displeased by the situation.

We glanced at each other, our looks saying, *she's great, Bette Davis is so great*. Our smiles were unfeasibly broad. The candles may have had something to do with it, but our flushed faces seemed to glow.

"Bette, will you do Margo Channing?" called out the usually reticent Hirata. It was the first time I'd heard her speaking in such a high voice. "Go on, please, Bette!"

Bette Davis grinned, put her hands to her waist, and delivered a stunning rendition of that famous line from movie history: "Fasten your seatbelts, it's going to be bumpy night."

Resounding applause and cheering filled the room. Sano, who had lived alone in this big house since losing his parents and wife unexpectedly, secretly wiped away tears as he wondered whether it had ever before seemed so full of life.

"So tell me then, why did you call on me? I'd give y'all a kiss, but I've just washed my hair."

Bette was apparently warming to us, and her manner seemed more familiar than before. We glanced at each other nervously—the time had come to get down to business. Nakamura, who'd we'd decided before would be the one to broach the subject, licked his lips and began.

"We've actually got a favor to ask you . . . "

Our little posse been brought together by Bette Davis. We were new fans of hers, all alike in having only discovered her in the twenty-first century. The five of us had come together gradually, after learning of each others' fandom on social media and other similar channels. The name for our group chat was "The Bette Lovers," with a heart emoji at the end.

All of us felt glad to have found like-minded souls. We were so happy to be able to share the sensation we got when watching Bette Davis, that power that seemed to charge through us. We were five people of assorted ages and genders, who felt that Bette Davis wasn't a relic from the past, but someone with huge relevance for the present day. We spoke with passion about her brilliance. Her mercurial range of expressions. Her powerful sense of individuality. That Medusa-like gaze. All those withering quotes, like, "When a man gives his opinion, he's a man. When a woman gives her opinion, she's a bitch." And as we watched that classic of hers, *What Ever Happened to Baby Jane?* we realized all of us had experienced the exact same sense of letdown.

"There's something we want to hear you say," Nakamura said finishing up, his voice trembling, at which point Sano took over.

"It's a loss for the human race that you didn't play the role. We beg you. If we can hear you say it just once, we'll be without regrets."

Our feelings were one, like soccer fans watching a penalty shoot-out, and we squeezed one another's hands and awaited Bette's answer.

"I can do anything at all, I'll have you know. Joan Crawford couldn't, but I can. What is it you want me to say? You've got me here, so I might as well. It ain't like they're keeping me busy in hell, that's for sure."

Overwhelmed by Bette Davis' generosity, our eyes welled up with tears, and we pronounced in unison,

"'I had a dream. A dream of Akira.'"

Bette Davis seemed confused. "Huh? Come again?"

"We want you to say, 'I had a dream. A dream of Akira,'" said Saitō, firmly. All of us stared pleadingly at Bette Davis.

When we'd seen her in *What Ever Happened to Baby Jane?* with her white lace dress, all of us had felt it: this was Kiyoko from *Akira*. She would have made a perfect Kiyoko. We wanted to see Bette Davis's Kiyoko, whatever it took. All five of us were desperate to experience the real-life Bette Davis saying this one line. Every time there was talk of making *Akira* into a live performance, we'd all experienced a great sense of disappointment. Ahh, if only Bette Davis was still alive! When the five of us were out drinking one night, we discovered our similar feelings on the matter and decided, right then and there, to make it happen.

"Please!"

"It's our dream!"

Apparently persuaded by our fervor, Bette Davis adopted a look of benevolence worthy of the Virgin Mary. This was, of course, the mark of her genius as an actor: she could play the bitches and the Madonnas and everything in between.

"I can't say I really get it . . . But sure, I'll do it."

With that, Bette Davis closed her big round eyes, as if falling into a state of deep concentration, then blinked them wide open. Without any hesitation, she pronounced the words, "I had a dream. A dream of Akira."

We all saw it, with total clarity. The figure of Bette Davis in a negligee, her hair loose. She had mastered Kiyoko, to a tee.

"Bravo!" The group let out a round of applause rapturous enough to set the house shaking. Some of us wolf-whistled. "Bravo!"

This incredible actor who had carved out a place in Hollywood history with her sheer talent shot us a radiant smile, chin pitched jauntily upwards, and then vanished.

After the medium had taken a taxi back to the hotel, all of us toasted with champagne. The glasses let out a pleasant clink. Leaning back into our chairs positioned around the round table, we basked in the lingering traces of Bette Davis' presence. That was our very best memory of her.

The Lip Balm Lake

I love when the time comes to buy a new pot of Rosebud Perfume Company lip balm. Prize off the round lid to the small turquoise container, with its pink pattern and the words "Smith's Menthol and Eucalyptus Balm" printed in black on top, and the world's smallest lake appears in front of your eyes.

The lake, the same color as frozen ice, is perfectly still. I'm always taken aback by its beauty. About the only thing that rivals it is the milk soap whose bar is imprinted with the image of a cow on one side, and the letters "C-O-W" on the other.

A small boat with small people onboard goes drifting across the small lake. The small people are holding small lace parasols. They wear small clothes with small puff sleeves and small bows. They carry small canes. The boat is loaded up with a small hamper, containing small sandwiches, boiled eggs and a bottle of wine. Through the green grove of trees they can see a small village in the distance.

Or maybe the ice-colored lake really is frozen over. There are small people skating on its surface. Their small faces are half-hidden by white fur hoods, and their small cheeks are glowing red. Their breath forms small white clouds. When they join their small hands swathed in thick mittens, it's as if they're holding hands with something that isn't quite human. Beneath the ice, the small fish are waiting for spring.

I have to stick my finger into this beautiful lake. I should just let my lips get chapped and cracked, I know. But I've got to do it. This is what I bought it for.

As soon as I touch the water's surface, the lake vanishes. I only need to make the faintest contact, only need to leave a fingerprint, and it's over. The small world disappears, indubitably, eternally. All that remains is the lip balm in the container, the refreshing menthol that tingles as it slides on. I never feel as boorish as I do this moment. Then I get over it, and use the lip balm.

How many more times will I be able to see this smallest of lakes while I'm still alive, I wonder?

The Death of Context

People die when they run out of air, but a text can live on without the air that gave it life, which is to say the context in which it was written. Texts live on even after their context is dead. Indeed, the fact that their context is no longer sometimes serves as a major selling point. I feel like that's the crucial difference between people and texts. I don't know whether that answers your question or not.

A Magic Spell

"I adjure you, stock cube! Dissolve as fast as you possibly can!"

Aoko Matsuda's One-Line Commentaries

The Android Whose Name Was Boy
This story evolved out of my thoughts about *Neon Genesis Evangelion*. It's now used in a Japanese high school textbook.

Bond
I thought it would be fun if all the Bond girls got together and enjoyed themselves.

Starry Night
I'd like people to look at Van Gogh's painting *The Starry Night* as they read this story.

English Composition No. 1
This whole series I wrote because I found the example sentences used in middle school English textbooks really odd. After finding out that people in America use the term "power suit" for a suit exuding confidence, I started wondering how people told the difference between power suits and other suits.

I Hate the Girls that You Like
This story was the starting point for my novel *The Sustainable Use of Our Souls*, which grew out of it.

Money
I wrote this after seeing the exhibition 'Pure Forms: Currencies of African Tribes' at Intermediateque in Tokyo Station.

You Are Not What You Eat
This story is what I ended up with when I flipped the English proverb, "You are what you eat" on its head.

My Secret Thrill
What inspired me to write this, I wonder?

God Must Be Stupid
Part of the "Cats are Brilliant" series.

Thoughts on Balthus' The Street
The first time that I saw this painting in a museum, I couldn't see this as anything other than a loaf of bread . . . Please look it up!

The National Anthem Gets It Bad
Maybe this isn't the case in every country, but in Japan the national anthem is seen as controversial, and big problems have erupted around people who refuse to sing it at various ceremonies. I wrote this story from the perspective of "Kimigayo," the Japanese national anthem, who falls in love with one such non-singer. I remember talking to someone from another country worried that writing this story would land me in jail . . .

The Sky Blue Hand
I want to wave at people, and have them wave back.

This Precious Opportunity
People have asked me if this kind of yogurt really exists—it does!

The Woman Dies
One morning I was half awake, breastfeeding my one-month-old baby and checking my my email with my free hand, when

I received the news that this story had been nominated for the Shirley Jackson Award. What a life, I remember thinking to myself, dazedly.

How to Transform from a Punk into a Girl-Next-Door/ How to Transform from a Girl-Next-Door into a Bad Girl
I like lipstick with intriguing names.

Victoria's Secret
Part I of the Adolescence Trilogy. I like adolescents!

The Year of No Wild Flowers
When I'm outside, I'm always on the lookout for wild flowers.

Murder in the Cat Cafe
Part of the "Cats are Brilliant" series.

We Can't Do It!
This story was inspired by the American World War II propaganda poster, featuring the slogan "We Can Do It!" above a woman flexing her bicep. I decided to see what happened if I negated it . . .

TOSHIBA Mellow #20 18-Watt
Don't you feel like this sometimes?

Hawai'i
This is a story written from the perspective of one of those items that no longer "sparks joy" . . . I've never been to Hawai'i either. I'd like to go.

The Purest Woman in the Kingdom
I remember being really fired up when I wrote this story, thinking like, yeah, I'm telling it how it is! I recently read a manga that

features "A Perfume That will Kill Subway Gropers Instantly Upon Smelling," and found myself wishing it really existed.

English Composition No. 2
I was very happy when I saw both these paintings at the Tate Britain.

Dear Doctor Spencer Reid
Part II of the Adolescence Trilogy. I wrote this story when I was going through a phase of being obsessed with Doctor Spencer Reid.

Life Is Like a Box of Chocolates
I saw *Forrest Gump* when I was in middle school.

Braids
I wrote this for a publication on Claire Denis put out by *Fireflies* Magazine, a Berlin magazine about contemporary cinema.

Messing Up the National Anthem
These national anthem stories came out of various thoughts I had on the Japanese national anthem and the Japanese "Hinomaru" flag. Both have a strong, conservative image, and I think I wrote these stories out of a wish to try and soften that a little.

Dissecting Misogyny
I've been asked if the narrator in this story was modelled on someone specific, and she is: it's Big Boo from *Orange is the New Black*.

Cage in a Cage
Once the idea for this occurred to me I had to go ahead and write it, but I slightly regret it now.

English Composition No. 3
I remember the English textbooks at middle school contained so many instances of the words "pop music." I also really love penguins.

The Masculine Touch
I wrote this out of the frustration that I was feeling about how often you saw phrases like "the feminine touch" and "the feminine perspective."

GABAN I / GABAN II
GABAN is the name of a Japanese food manufacturer. I'm obsessed with the jars of maraschino cherries in syrup that they produce. As far as I know, they come in two color variations.

To You, Sleeping in an Armory
This story came out of my fear of war.

CV
I wrote this for an anthology whose theme was "Decade."

Baseball Player Soup
Apparently it was after reading this story that Fireflies Press in Berlin thought I'd make a good contributor to the Claire Denis issue.

Curtain of Celebration
I wrote this for the "Northern Lights" issue of *TRANSIT* Magazine.

Remembering Technology
I wrote this for the "Technology" issue of *IMA* Magazine.

Bird Strike!
I wrote this because I found it so heartbreaking to think of birds being killed in bird strikes.

The National Anthem Goes to New York
I wanted to give the National Anthem a vacation.

Flora
Part III of the Adolescence Trilogy.

Twenty-First Century Tinkerbell
This grew out of the thought that if Tinkerbell existed in the present, she probably wouldn't be hanging around with Peter Pan, but off doing her own thing.

The Start of the Weekend
The Japanese consumption tax rate went up from 8% to 10% between the hardback and paperback versions of this book, so I altered the costs accordingly.

Reflection
I like mysteries, but as I'm reading I'm always astonished by how observant the detectives are.

When the Girl Broke Up with Her Boyfriend
There was a guy who read this and said to me, I think this is like a female thing, but I can assure you that this is not what this story's about.

A Father and His Back
I wrote this for the "Father And Son" issue of *MONKEY* Magazine.

Youth and Sadness
This is one of my favorite flower meanings.

Bette Davis
I'm a big Bette Davis fan too.

The Lip Balm Lake
This lake really is beautiful.

The Death of Context
This story was conceived out of the fact that in Japanese, the word for context (bunmyaku, 文脈) contains the word for pulse (myaku, 脈). It just kind of popped into my head.

A Magic Spell
I don't ever want to stop feeling a sense of wonder in my daily life.